FRI<u>EN</u>D

Khadija Styles

DEDICATION

I would like to dedicate my book to my amazing editor, Alexia McLean for her dedication and time while editing my first novel. She is a woman of many talents; great mother, Paralegal, wife and confidante. Her expertise has been a true blessing during my journey to becoming an author.

Table of Contents

CHAPTER 1: THE START

In this generation the word 'friend' has completely lost its true meaning and value. We easily befriend someone because we can have fun with them, or to be politically correct, to "Turn up" or "Get it lit" with. However, when it's time to confide in a so called 'friend' about meaningful things going on in your life, you have to be very careful with whom you tell because there seems to be no such thing as privacy between two individuals anymore. Trust me, I know. I've have had my fair share of back-stabbers and double-crossers, and those were people I would have never thought would betray my confidence. But, for whatever reason, we keep forgiving these people and allowing them back into our lives to hurt us just because we want to be accepted and not left out of the group. I'm sure many people can relate to having one or two friends do them wrong in the past; but, you know what they say, keep your friends close and your 'frenemies' closer. Unfortunately for me, I've had to learn to do so with my group of friends.

Not all of them were untrustworthy, but the ones that were, just needed a keener eye kept on them as their sneaky, conniving ways led me to question their character. Our crew consisted of Hazel Nelson, the twins - Jenelle and Jayna Dale, the Twins, Cora Lendo, Donna Stone, and Leena White. And just who am I you're wondering? I'm Bonnie Heart. We've all been best friends since elementary school, with the exception of Donna whom we met our first year of high school, but she fit right in with her slim figure, enticing green eyes and her wild ways. Some of our friendships didn't start out in the best way, simply due to the fact that we all have strong personalities; meaning, our first interactions weren't very friendly ones.

I met Jenelle and Jayna in senior kindergarten, and we used to live in the same building before my parents bought a house in the suburbs. As they got older, they grew beautifully into their flawless caramel complexions which made so many girls full of envy. Their big beautiful bright eyes made them seem innocent but they were far from innocent. Jenelle had a mole on her top lip which was the only way you could tell them apart, besides their personalities. Jenelle is boy crazy and Jayna loves the ladies and was damn good at getting them and even turning some straight girls out.

We met Hazel when she enrolled at Corsair Public School in the middle of the 4th grade. Even with her beautiful hazel eyes, which is how she got her name, Hazel was made fun of often by her classmates because she had buck teeth that surpassed her bottom lip - luckily, she grew out of that. We became friends when I stood up for her against the mean girls, which of course included the twins. Hazel had light brown hair that complimented her skin but lacked shape, to the point she has been contemplating surgery since the tender age of thirteen. Fortunately, her face made up for her lack of assets. Hazel was fun to be around, but was an attention seeker. If she knew a guy was into one of her friends she would all of a sudden become somewhat interested in them and pursue them to seek interest in her. I guess because we were much younger, we didn't think much of it at the time because she was our girl; but that would eventually change.

Cora and Lena went to the public elementary school around the corner from us. As soon as the 8th grade hit, we were allowed to go to the mall for lunch with a written permission form from our parents; and, that's when we met the both of them. They made fun of Jayna because she was looking at a girl in a more romantic way. We got into a fight, and somehow became friends after that. As our friendship grew and we all attended high school together, Cora emerged as the peacemaker. Her beliefs and mind frame made her so pleasant to be around. Another beautiful thing was her face. She's the tall model looking type, which caught the attention of many but Cora never accepted anyone's advances. With all her beauty, her heart was the most beautiful thing about her. Leena, on the other hand, is someone who we like to call book-smart, but so stupid when it comes to the real world, and she never learns from her mistakes. She was the smallest out of all of us but had the loudest voice. She was the craziest Latina girl I've ever met, basically bipolar, but she was fun to be around and was always the life of the party.

Then there's me… I like to call myself dark and lovely due to my milk chocolate skin, hour glass frame and full of life attitude. Of course as a kid I looked a lot different; like I said, we all have our awkward faze. I definitely evolved from a nerdy caterpillar to a lovely butterfly.

For me, turning eighteen and about to graduate and enter the real world made me really start to re-examine what I wanted out of life. The intense partying, drinking, smoking, even some of us having sex, was not how I wanted to continue living my life. For some, when you're approaching early adulthood and start having aspirations and goals you want to pursue, it doesn't always sit well with everyone, especially those who aren't ready to make the same changes, and are selfishly not ready for you to leave the same partying lifestyle that you have all become accustomed to. Some friends will start to become envious, and may even try to discourage you and/or make you doubt yourself. Secretly, they are hoping that you'll fail. They usually act this way because they're not happy with where they are in life. Simply put, if they're not chasing their dreams or if nothing is going well for them, how dare you try to prosper before they get it together. It's messed up how your so called 'friends' would silently hope for you to fail just because they're not on the same page. Believe me when I say it, we all have frenemies, some of us just don't know it yet. One day you'll realize who these people are, and understand the reason why there's an 'end' in 'friend'.

CHAPTER 2: THROUGH THICK AND THIN

High school is like an empire of its own. The Principal and the Vice-Principal are the government, the teachers are law enforcement and the students are the citizens. The citizens of "H.S." are either making a difference or breaking the law - translation, you're either doing your work and studying focusing on graduation, or spending time on trying to be "cool," skipping classes, fucking or sucking someone on the stairwell, or planning to whoop someone's ass for fucking your man or wifey. There was a lot to deal with in high school but I enjoyed it, the good and the bad and there was a fair mix of both. High school is where you experience a lot of firsts; your first crush, first kiss, as well as your first sexual encounter. For high school students, sex was never like how they portrayed it in movies. It was dramatic, not at all pleasurable, and it never stayed just between the two people involved in the act. If you lost your virginity or just randomly hooked-up with someone, you better believe the whole school was going to be talking about it the following school day. High school would either make you or break you - only the strong survived.

Hazel, Donna and I attended Kingston Secondary School. Hazel and I met in elementary school, and we both became friends with Donna in high school. Donna knew a lot of older people and showed us around after her and Hazel finally settled their feud of who was better looking. Like I said, it was completely unexpected for our group to have become friends. At first, Donna disliked Hazel because they were both red bone girls, which made Donna feel intimidated by her being more desirable by our mannish peers; and of course, the fact that everyone was saying that Donna had competition added fuel to the fire. Donna didn't like that at all so she tried to find something to beef about with Hazel. What Donna didn't know was that Hazel wasn't someone you can push over, if you step to her she will make you think twice about stepping to her ever again. As much as Hazel was fun to be around, she had a nasty attitude that we all hated. A lot of the times no one said anything because it would escalate into something bigger and no one wanted that, especially if we're all supposed to be best friends. One day, Donna learned just how nasty Hazel could be. She tried to bring up some bullshit story about Hazel talking about her, which Hazel was definitely not having and gave Donna a piece of her mind. Hazel sized up Donna in front of the whole school and from then on, all three of us have been tighter than ever. Although we were tight there was something a little off about Donna, she seemed too nice, but only time would tell. Donna noticed how much Hazel would flirt with Pay at times but she knew like everyone else in the group that Hazel wouldn't go there seeing that she had a man too. The funny thing was, that as soon as Pay and Donna started getting serious, Hazel confessed to me that she was kind of feeling him, but since she was still unsure about her feelings for Pay, we kept that little secret between her and I. Uncertain feelings are harmless, right? I did feel like I was being a bad friend to Donna by not telling her, but knowing Hazel first, I felt more of an obligation to her to keep her secret so I did, but we all know secrets come to light, eventually.

Since we were fifteen we were going to 19 and over clubs, drinking, smoking weed every weekend and sometimes on weekdays, our crew was inseparable. Plus, Pay had his own spot so we had no supervision which lead us to do whatever we wanted whenever we wanted. It was a teen's perfect life but it was not always fun and games, especially when there was alcohol involved. When a group of people were intoxicated, anything could happen, and I mean anything, but I'll get into that a little bit later. Donna and Pay's little fling started to turn real serious and I can tell Hazel didn't like it sometimes she showcased a bit of jealousy and as that jealousy grew she started to confess her feelings for Pay even more. Although Hazel didn't tell anyone else in the group besides myself, it was starting to become obvious to others in the group, but no one said anything until we started going to Pay's house more and more without Donna. Donna would call Hazel and ask her what she was up to, and she would lie and say she had other things to do- those other things involved Donna's man and the rest of the crew being witnesses to their dirty little secret. We would all go out and party and Hazel would be all up on Pay, drunk as fuck. If you didn't know the crew, you would think Hazel and Pay were a couple, and I don't think Pay seemed to mind because it didn't look like he was thinking about Donna one bit. Hazel and Pay's relationship evolved from just an innocent friendship to harmless flirting (once Donna and Pay started dating), to what was now a relationship as a careless couple in love who didn't trouble themselves about what anyone else thought even though they both knew what they were doing was wrong and would hurt Donna. I mean they would fight like they were a couple and make-out like they were lovers. It was horrible, yet no one addressed the situation, with Hazel being our friend and all, we just went with the flow, so I guess we weren't in any position to judge. I felt that we were all being selfish because if Donna found out the truth about their relationship and our involvement (by knowing what was going on and not even dropping so much as a hint to her), the fun in our crew would be over. Everyone would be forced to choose sides and go our separate ways, and no one wanted that. I know, I know, that's so fucked up. I use to question, what if it was me? What if one of my own friends was messing around with someone that I loved and everybody knew about it but me, and was smiling in my face like everything was gravy; I would be so heartbroken. I could only imagine how Donna would feel because she fell in love with Pay fast and hard. After a year of dating, ups and downs, and speculations that Hazel and Pay had something going on, she stilled loved him dearly and she wasn't going to let go of him anytime soon. He could be fucking someone right in front of her and she would turn a blind eye just so she could justify being with him. It was sad but true. Things took a turn for the worst when Donna became pregnant with Pay's baby. We all thought she got pregnant on purpose because Pay got his other girl pregnant, yes - Hazel wasn't the only girl he was messing around with - Zia was his first wifey. The trigger however, was Donna getting pregnant for Pay, as soon as Hazel found out, she turned up the heat on their "little affair" fast.

Pay and Hazel were quite similar though. Even though Hazel was messing around with Pay and was anxious to intensify their relationship now that she felt as if Donna had "one upped" her, she also had a man, believe it or not The thing was, no one liked Hazel's man Leon, because he was a straight up asshole. He treated Hazel like shit but she always took him back without hesitation. It wasn't even like he was sexy, he was beyond average but he had money, a very sexy voice and a long, strong dick as she told everyone. She always bragged that the sex between them was great. I guess it was good enough for her to take hits like a man and be cheated on left, right and center. She was literally at the doctor's office every week. Jayna used to tell her to "Be careful, because one day he's going to give you something you won't be able to cure." It may have sounded like a bitch thing to say but Jayna hated Leon the most and did not shy away from telling the truth as she saw fit. She couldn't stand how he treated Hazel and hated that she kept going back to him. We all gave her "the talk" that she could do better but that didn't help. The more that Hazel and Leon's relationship became strained, the more Hazel turned to Pay for attention. Before Pay and Donna got together, Pay only paid Hazel attention when she wanted some foreplay. What man as young as Pay would turn down pussy? Pay made her feel special while Leon's idea of treating Hazel special was labeling her as his girl and buying her nice things every time he put a bruise on her body. There were a lot of bruises, but the ones you were able to see never compared to the ones you couldn't see. It was no life for a beautiful teenager to live, but there's something about your first. It's as if you are compelled to stay with the guy you lost your virginity to. A lot of girls do this but most are smart enough to leave when shit hits the fan, but not Hazel. As smart as she was, she made stupid choices when it came to love and this was one of many, but it didn't top what was about to happen.

Over the March break, Hazel and Leon got into a horrible fight and stopped talking for a couple weeks, which of course only brought Pay and Hazel closer, much closer than they have ever been. One night our crew, not including Donna, was chilling at my house when my parents went on a business trip and my sisters were at a friend's house for the night. The house was packed with liquor and Pay brought weed to last for days! We had the music playing so loud that my neighbor came over to ask if we could turn it down a few times. It was a normal night besides the fact that everybody seemed to be horny as ever! Cora and Dready were getting cozy in the basement, Jenelle went to go meet one of her "boo's" at the plaza by my house, Jayna was having phone sex with one of her girls in the downstairs washroom, and Coolie Boy and I were just chilling on the couch cuddled up while we smoked a joint. Coolie Boy and I never had anything going on but he was never shy about expressing his feelings for me even though he knew that I was not interested. I had my eye on Sean. He was no good but he was the only one I had any interest in at the time. Sean played basketball and was a mama's boy, but he was handsome. I wanted him so bad but he had a main girl already. Before I found out about his relationship status we had a make-out session and bit of kitty sucking, but I'm not about being a side

9

chick, where's the respect in that. If I was going to get any further with a guy other than them pleasuring me, he would have to be worth it. Now I'm no goodie too shoes, but I messed around with a few cuties but none of them got to eat the whole cake. I was still a virgin, but that doesn't mean that they never tried to take it, they just didn't succeed. It felt good to say no one has had me in that way. I wanted to lose my virginity when I felt that I finally had mutual love and respect with a man that would actually appreciate me for my mind as well as my body, but at the moment, no one was a potential candidate. As Hazel couldn't control her sexual tension that was building up for Pay, and I'm sure Pay didn't mind because he was dying to feel what Hazel's pussy was all about. With all the fooling around they did, I'm surprised they didn't get in on sooner. It had just been major foreplay between the two of them; fingering, titty sucking, hand jobs and all that good stuff, but tonight they both wanted to take it to the next level. After about an hour, Jenelle came back to my house, and everyone else but Hazel and Pay joined Coolie Boy and I in the living room to just chill while the movie played in the background. Hazel and Pay were still in my guestroom, but a few minutes later, Hazel ran out of the room dramatically crying and the girls and I ran to her aid. We went outside on my verandah and she started to explain what happened in the room. "What did I do?! Leon is going to hate me; I can't believe we fucked!" The rest of us stood there all thinking the same thing- it was destined to happen. Shit, we were all surprised to hear that this was their first time. As she cried we tried to console her, although she was wrong and we all knew it, but still, we stood by her side to comfort her. After we all agreed not to utter a word about it to anyone, they all got their stuff, went home and acted like nothing happened.

The next day at school Hazel didn't show up because she had a terrible hangover, and since the rest of the crew didn't attend our high school, I was forced to act normal when I saw

Donna. She asked me what I did the previous night and that's when the guilt began to eat away at me. To hide such a secret from someone who I called a best friend was so difficult. I felt horrible because I knew I betrayed Donna's trust and possibly ruined our friendship by keeping this from her. After school I went over to Hazel's to check on her and wasn't surprised that not only did she look like shit but that she felt like it too. I even had to lie to Donna again and tell her I was going out with my sisters so she wouldn't want to come with me to Hazel's. Hazel and I went to her room to talk and she immediately sat on her bed and began to cry. Even though she was wrong for what she did, I couldn't help but feel bad for her. She had to find a way to tell Leon and Donna. "I fucked up so bad. How am I going to tell Leon?" I waited for her to say how she was planning to tell Donna, but all she could talk about was how she was going tell her cheating ass boyfriend?! It made me question if she even cared about Donna at all. It started to bother me so much that I asked, "When are you going to tell Donna?" She looked at me and said, "I don't know. I kind of don't want to tell her." I literally sat there with my mouth open. With the expression on my face she had to have known what I was thinking. "Personally I think you should tell her; it will only get worse if you say nothing at all. Just think if she hears it from someone else how much worse it can get," I stated. She looked at me and asked, "Do you plan on telling her?" "It's not my business to talk about. That's for you and Pay to confess to her. I would only cause bigger problems if I did," I replied. Hazel sighed in relief. All I wanted to do was show her that keeping this from Donna would not end well for anyone, especially for her, but she clearly had her mind made up and for some reason I felt as though she didn't want to tell Donna the truth because she wanted to continue to sleep with Pay. Hazel's phone rang and we both looked down to see that it was Pay calling. I looked at her and saw nothing but happiness in her eyes as she stared at his name on her phone. She answered his call with a baby doll voice- the one you do when your man calls. I heard Pay ask Hazel how she was doing and her response was "good." Good? I repeated in my head wondering why I was even there in the first place when all they were discussing was hooking up later that night. I looked around the room is such disbelief that she was talking like this, especially right in front of me. I know that Hazel and I were the closest out of the group, so she was very comfortable saying things to me that she wouldn't say to the rest of the girls out of fear of being judged I guess, but this was about something more than your average gossip. Knowing that they were actually going to continue their treachery, a part of me knew I was still going to ride with her, through thick and thin, but she could never say that I didn't warn her. Although I really wanted to tell Donna, it just wasn't my place to say anything, at least that's how I felt and rationalized it.

After Hazel hung up with Pay, she then got some balls and called Leon to confess. He called her every name in the book and shouted, "Don't you ever call me again!" He hung up on her and she actually tried to call him about a hundred times, but he never answered. She cried for a bit and still went to fuck Pay later that night. For weeks this went on until Donna called me out of the blue, "Hi Donna. What's up?" I asked. "Can I ask you a question?" She gave me no time to even say yes, and carried on, "Why didn't you tell me that Hazel and Pay were fucking behind my back?" I was at a standstill. I replied "I wanted to but that was for Pay and Hazel to tell you, it wasn't my place." Donna started to cry and I started to feel sick to my stomach. I prayed it was a dream but I knew that the truth was going to come out sooner or later. "I'm sorry Donna… I really am, and you have every reason to be mad with me but…" Donna cut me off cold, "But what if it was you?"

CHAPTER 3: TRUST ISSUES

After Donna found out the truth about Pay and Hazel having sex, people started to talk. The whispers accompanied by the impolite looks while Hazel walked down the hallways as school began, and it didn't faze Hazel one bit. She was still chilling with Pay as usual, maybe even a lot more if you ask me. A week later, Hazel turned to me while we were sitting in the cafe and said, "I don't know what it is, but something just excites me about having everybody speculate if we're still screwing behind Donna's back while we deny it. It makes the sex more exciting." I couldn't believe my ears. I just shook my head and thought to myself that she truly has no shame in her game. I know Hazel and I are closer than everybody else in the group but even I would expect some censoring out of respect that she knows that I care about Donna and wanted to work on rebuilding our trust. As she sat there with a grin on her face, I quickly changed the subject, "So...What did you do last night?" She looked at me and chuckled. "I was with Pay." I rolled my eyes thinking I would get away from hearing about her and Pay's sexcapades. We went to dinner and saw a movie..." she then burst out in laughter. I shook my head again and smirked, just guessing what she was going to say. Hazel continued trying to contain herself, "We had sex in the theatre and it was amazing! We sat all the way at the back and there were a few people in the theatre. I started to rub on his dick, while he kissed on my neck, giving me hickies, which started to get the both of us horny. He then slid his two fingers up my skirt, and I wasn't even wearing underwear - that made him super excited. I hitched up my skirt and slid onto his lap, his penis was at attention, ready for my goods. He gripped my thighs so tight as I was riding him, pulling me down going

13

deep inside of me. It was so hard to control my moaning, I was getting so loud that at one point a couple sitting a few rows before us looked back- they knew what we were doing," she smirked. "Anyways," I quickly interrupted Hazel before she continued tell me her night as a pornstar." "I get it, you fucked. I don't need nor want to hear the play by play with you and Pay. Ok? Thanks." Hazel finished with a smile on her face portraying her enjoyment of her affair with Pay. I asked, "You used a condom, right?" She smiled and said nothing. "Are you crazy?!" I shouted, forgetting where we were. "What if you get pregnant for him? Donna's pregnant for him right now and he just had a baby with Zia." Hazel replied, "Calm down Bonnie, I'm on the pill." I was so disappointed in her. She had her ways but this was just too much, she was being disrespectful on every level. Hazel was acting as if she never heard of the saying "What goes around comes around," and by the looks of her situation, her karma was sure going to be a big bitch.

I was supposed to go shopping with Hazel and Cora the following day, but with all the drama I just wanted to chill and smoke a spliff at home. I called up my weed man Ray and was on cloud 9 an hour later. I chilled out with my sisters, chowed down on some junk food, and made jokes all day. It felt good to just have a good laugh with no drama. Later on I took a nap and woke up a few hours later surprised to see thirty-five missed calls from Hazel. You would have thought I was her man judging by the amount of times she called me; plus, she left four rude ass messages on my phone asking what kind of friend I was when she needed me at a time like this - Hazel was known to be melodramatic. As soon as I pressed the send button to call her back my doorbell rang. I heard yelling as I was walking down the stairs to the door, which sounded like a group of people having a disagreement. I looked through my window only to see Cora, Leena, Hazel and the twins on my porch and they didn't look happy. I opened the door and asked,

"What's up y'all?" Everybody answered expect Hazel. She gave me a dirty look when she came in, talking on her phone about the drama that just happened. Cora then started to explain what all the hype was about. "We were at the mall shopping and decided to grab something to eat in the food court. We found a table and sat down, and not even 10 seconds into eating Donna, her cousins and a few of their friends came up and started to cuss Hazel about sleeping with Pay. Donna didn't say much, it was all Donna's butch ass cousin and her manly looking friends." Then the twins started to get all hype and continued, "Hazel got all up in Donna's cousin's face and said - "Fuck you bitch! If I was fucking him, what you gonna do?" "Donna must have grown some balls because she moved in and slapped the shit out of Hazel," Jayna laughed. Hazel entered the room pissed, "Where the fuck were you Bonnie? I called you a million times. I needed you." "So, I'm psychic now? How the hell was I supposed to know that you were in some kind of trouble? I was sleeping and had my phone on silent. How does that make me a bad friend?" I snapped back at her. She stood there in silence for a bit, which she never does because her ass always had something to say. "I'm always there for you, wherever, whenever and whatever, and you know that, so don't come at me with any bullshit!" I just wasn't in the mood for any drama and quite frankly, Hazel needed a reality check. Hazel's phone rang and she walked off to talk to Pay who was on the other end. Jayna, still pumped with adrenaline from the fight but in, "Anyways, Donna kept slapping Hazel in the face so we all had to jump in. Leena, Jayna and I were fighting their friends and Hazel had her hands full with both Donna and her cousin. She was handling herself for a bit until she got kicked in her back and Donna's cousin punched her in her rib cage. Cora was trying to be the mediator and break up the fight but that did not work at all!" All I could think to myself was that two girls fighting over a dude was never a good thing and would only end up bad. It's an ongoing and senseless feud. Leena then continued to tell the story. "Then Donna's cousin threw Hazel on one of the tables at the food court and continued to punch her shamelessly. Security came rushing in and everyone scattered like roaches do when you turn on the lights. Random people just started to laugh." Anyone that knew how Hazel felt about being embarrassed knows that got to her the most, and the fact that she couldn't get a hold of me made her even more furious. Hazel then interrupted Leena, "It's kind of weird to me that you were supposed to be there and decided not to come, Bonnie. It's like you knew something was going to go down or maybe you were even a part of the setup?" I replied with rage in my eyes, "Are you fucking crazy?! Why would I do that? What would I get out of it? It's not like I got to see you get your ass whipped, which you brought on yourself by the way! If I was a part of anything, I would have told Donna about you and Pay the first time you hooked up with him behind her back!" Everyone looked at me as if they were shocked at what I said, but I didn't care, it was true. I was so appalled that she would even make such accusations against me when I have always kept her dirty little secrets to myself. Hazel then picked up her stuff and left. The rest of our crew followed her of course. I slammed my door and went to roll a spliff to relax my nerves. I was so heated; I probably smoked five spliff's by the end of the night. The next day I went to school and saw Hazel at her locker. "You still think I had something to do with the fight?" She looked at me and said "No," as she put her head down. "I just feel like I can't trust anyone after the whole thing with Pay and I. I feel like I have to have my guard up all the time, even towards my own friends, but I know that's my fault. I know I'm wrong for what I did to Donna but... Pay was giving me the attention that Leon wasn't and I just got caught up in the hype." As Hazel tried to hold back her tears I gave her a huge. Donna then walked by and looked at Hazel and I and walked off. I felt like I was in the middle more than the rest of the girls because I went to school with both of them and I was closest to both of them as well. I started to develop a complex of my own as I didn't feel like a true friend.

After school was finished, Hazel went home and I went to Donna's to talk about the fight. She invited me in but it didn't seem like she really wanted me there, I know she felt as if she couldn't trust me because I was so close to Hazel, and even though Hazel was the one in the wrong, she didn't understand why I was so empathetic towards her. As soon as we sat down in the kitchen, Donna got straight to the point. "I don't understand how you still rock with Hazel? She fucked my man and everybody is running to her seeing if she's ok, when I'm the one who was hurt and betrayed by one of my best friends and man. What is it going to take for you guys to see that this chick has fucking issues? Maybe you guys will finally see her for who she is when she fucks your man. Does anyone even care that I'm pregnant for Pay right now? I'm stressed out; I can't eat, sleep or even think straight. I feel like I'm losing it." I looked down on the floor and wished I didn't even come over in the first place, but I owed it to her. "I am truly sorry Donna, and I know that saying it will never express how terrible I feel for not telling you and betraying our trust. I know it's even harder hearing that I'm sorry while I'm still friends with Hazel. I could never imagine how you feel, no matter how hard I try to put myself in your position. I know you still love Pay even after what happened. He's the father of your child. I don't even feel like I'm a true friend to you after all of this. I know I could never redeem myself as your friend. Honestly, I don't even feel like you should be my friend." She then sat down beside me and said, "Even though you're right, I know you're a good person, you just felt stuck in the middle of everything. You've been best friends with Hazel for many years, who was I to think that you would be more loyal to me than her. All I wanted was to be friends with you guys. You're fun to be around and accept my craziness." We both looked at each other and laughed. "I'm just really hurt right now, but I appreciate you coming to see me. Out of everyone, you're the only one out of our crew that has even apologized to me. I know you mean well Bonnie." I smiled and hugged her. I had to ask, "Who told you?" She replied, "Pay did. We had sex one night and after that I felt uncomfortable down there, so I went to the doctor's office and they told me that I had a STI. I told Pay and he told me that the last and only person he had unprotected sex with was Hazel." I was shocked and felt even worse because Donna was pregnant and had to be put on antibiotics. Donna continued, "I know Pay has cheated on me before but he had always used protection with those hoes, the fact that he didn't use protection with Hazel makes me think it's more than just a sex thing, I feel like he wants to be with her, which makes me even more sick to my stomach just thinking about it. They could still be fucking for all I know." I instantly put my game face on because I knew they were still fucking but if I said anything after that ass whopping Donna put on Hazel, Donna would probably just get her cousin to kill her. I'm sure any pregnant woman that found out her friend not only fucked her man but was still fucking him even after being found out, would also put a hit out on that ass, especially with all of their hormones out of whack. My relationship with Hazel and Donna started feeling more like I was working two full-time jobs than just having a normal teenage friendship. It seemed like it was easier having both of them hate me and going my own separate way then trying to keep up appearances. Donna's phone rang and it was Pay calling to take her out to dinner that night, but I knew that Hazel mentioned that she was meeting up with Pay later on that night. Looks like Pay is the only one that had it 'easy breezy'. He had both of these chicks going back and forth fighting for his yellow dick. I guess that shit must be golden, because they acted like it had more value than their pride and was the only one available. With all the lies and betrayal, I knew it was only a matter of time before someone ended up hurt, and I mean more hurt than they could ever imagine. It's like my mom says, those that don't learn from their mistakes shall feel the pain.

I left Donna's house with unresolved feelings, but I had to put it all out of my head, for awhile anyway, to catch up on all the work I've been putting off since all this mess went down. As I pushed my key in my door I got a call from Cora saying Hazel was in the hospital. She explained that Leon was waiting outside of her house when she got home after school because he said that they needed to talk. Leon was already a crazy person, so for Hazel to just allow him in her house thinking he had forgiven her after fucking Pay was stupid. I told Cora to meet me at the hospital and then I called up Jayna and Jenelle to pick me up so we could head over to see Hazel since they lived the closest to me. We arrived at the hospital within twenty minutes and ran to the receptionist. "What room is Hazel Nelson in?" The nurse replied, "You guys are going to have to wait awhile, the doctor is still examining her." Jenelle and Jayna went outside for a cigarette and I headed for the waiting room. Cora was already there with Leena and Ms. Nelson, and I could tell we were all thinking the worst. What could Leon have done to her that would send her to the hospital? What if she was on life support, or poured acid on her; I've heard plenty of stories of crazy ex's trying to kill their women. I didn't know what to think. My mind was everywhere; I just wanted to know that my friend was ok. When the doctor finally came out and told us we could see her, we all hurried to her room. Hazel was lying on the bed with cuts and bruises all over her arms, but what had us in shock was the patch over her left eye. She was happy to see us but you could see the sadness in her face. Hazel began to cry, "Why did this have to happen to me." Hazel was a beautiful girl and now she would have to live with a permanent deep cut over her left eye and scars that would never heal on the inside.

I asked her what happened, and she began to tell the horrifying story. "I was headed home and as I approached my driveway I saw Leon. I automatically felt uneasy, especially since I haven't spoken to him since I told him about Pay and I sleeping together. He asked me if we could go inside and talk, and even though I was hesitant, I let him in. It's like I knew something was about to happen but because I've been trying to get Leon to talk to me for so long and the fact the he was willing to, I said yes. We walked in my house and as soon as I shut the door…" Hazel paused for a moment and then continued, "He punched me in the face and I fell to the ground and he started kicking me, and kicking me and kicking me. I cried and begged him to stop. He then dragged me to the living room and kicked me in my chest and through me on the sofa. Leon back handed me in my face so hard, my filling came out and I fell onto the ground. I thought he would stop after he saw the blood on my face but it only got worse. As I lay on the floor crying and in pain, he went to the kitchen and got a knife. I thought he was going to kill me. I tried to run to the washroom but he tripped me and I hit the ground face first. He then turned me around and sat on top of me. He said, "I'm the only one that should have fucked you, how could you do this to us. You think because you're pretty you can fuck around on me? Huh? You think anyone is going to fuck you like me. As he insulted me, he slapped me around some more and then he put the knife to my face. I was terrified and knew I had to do something. I lifted my right leg to knee him in his balls, but as I did that I felt a sharp pain on my face. The knife had slit my left eyebrow and half of my eyelid. The blood started running down my face and I pushed him off me and ran out my house shouting for help. Leon ran out and drove away in his car. My neighbor came out to help me and called the police and my mother. The ambulance came, and that's how I got here." We all stood there in shock. Cora and Leena were crying, and Jayna and Jenelle looked like they were going to call up

Pookie to tell him it's on. I was speechless. I knew this whole situation was going to blow up in her face, but I didn't expect all of this. Hazel almost died because of a stupid decision she made out of jealousy and her need for attention. I would have never imagined it getting to this point. We all stayed at the hospital with Hazel, even Donna came and they had a heart to heart. Donna was still mad about everything but she wasn't an evil person. She felt really bad about what happened to Hazel. We all slept at the hospital with Hazel, afraid that Leon would come back to finish what he started.

The following morning the doctor came in to examine Hazel again and determined that she would have to stay for a few more days. We were all really saddened by everything that happened, but we had to go and told Hazel we would be back to visit her in a couple of days. I went back to the hospital later that evening. I asked Hazel how she was feeling. "I'm feeling better. My body is still sore but I'll bounce back. My face on the other hand..." Hazel then said that she had left out a part of the story that she didn't want to mention in front of the girls. I laid down beside her on the hospital bed as she began to tell me the part she had left out. "When Leon tripped me to the ground and was saying all that crazy shit he began to cut my clothes off. I tried to fight him but he was so strong. As he ripped off my clothes he then cut my underwear off he began to rape me, but it didn't seem like he was raping me, it was more like he was making love to me. He was kissing my neck and sucking my breasts softly. I kind of forgot what was even happening. He was telling me he loved me and wanted me to have his baby. As twisted as it sounds, I began to enjoy it and told him I loved him too. It was aggressive but passionate at the same time. He didn't have a condom on and as he was about to cum, he said he wanted me to have his baby and kept forcing himself on me. After he came inside of me, he made me lay there for a few minutes so I couldn't go to the bathroom to greater his chances of getting me pregnant. That was when he put the knife to my face." I had a look on my face like, bitch, the man was trying to kill you! She looked at me and was clearly ashamed, but she had to tell someone I guess. I said "Did you take the morning after pill? She looked away and said, "I don't want to. I feel like I owe Leon for cheating on him. I feel like if I do have his baby, it will make everything better." I stood up and demanded her to take the pill, "Hazel, are you insane? What makes you think you owe Leon anything? Having a child for him will only make matters worse. He's just going to think he owns you and try to control you more than he already does!" She replied, "I just want him to trust me again Bonnie, to love me how he used to love me." "A baby will not change anything," I exclaimed boldly; but it seemed as if Hazel already had her mind made up, she was having his baby no matter what anyone said.

CHAPTER 4: FIRST TIME

The next few months were a breath of fresh air. Donna and Hazel started to work on their friendship, I'm assuming because Donna no longer thought of Hazel as a threat, with her having Leon's baby and all, she figured Hazel wouldn't have time to sleep around with Pay. Donna was due in two months and Hazel was in her second trimester. Donna and Pay were also working on rebuilding the trust in their relationship. As for me, I felt much relief that I no longer had to deal with feeling guilty of being both of their friends when they were at war. It seemed as if Hazel's ass whooping from Leon was a blessing in disguise, as bad as that may sound. Everyone was getting along - we were drama free for once! However, I knew deep down that the peace in our crew was not going to last for long, but until then, I was going to enjoy the drama free life. With Donna and Hazel getting their pregnant bond on, the rest of the crew was still up to the same things; living our lives the way teens do, drinking, smoking and hitting up the hottest parties in town. School was finally out and it was time to play. We loved summer-time because we were able to spend more time with each other, have wild nights and do all the things careless free-spirited teenage girls do. To celebrate the start of summer, Cora, Jayna, Jenelle, Leena and I went out to club Melo, where the vibes are right and the guys are fine. As much as I love to look at a good piece of eye candy, I still didn't want to get involved with anyone. I just didn't trust them and I wasn't about getting hurt, even though secretly, I would have liked to be in a loving relationship. Cora and I were the only virgins out of our crew. I was waiting to give myself to someone who was truly worthy of respecting my mind, body and soul. As much as I wanted that, I knew I wasn't going to find that guy in the club.

Club Melo was popping tonight. My girls and I were drinking and dancing the night away, just having a really good time. I noticed that this fine brother who had been staring at me for a while was moving closer and closer my way. I was enjoying the vibes so much I just kept dancing with my eyes closed and one hand on my waist. I felt someone softly place their hand on top of mine, so I opened my eyes quickly and looked behind me, only to realize that it was the same guy that was watching me the entire night. He whispered in my ear, "My name is Drew and I like you." We both laughed because his line was corny as hell and he knew it too. "Excuse me for my corny line, but I'm feeling nice and I couldn't think of anything else to say that would get your attention. I thought if I could make you laugh you would let me have the pleasure of getting to know you better." I looked at him and said with a smile, "Yes, that was corny, but I do like to laugh so I guess I'll give you five minutes of my time and start with my name - Bonnie." The lights then came on and revealed how handsome Drew really was. He was about 5'10, brown eyes with long eyelashes, dark chocolate skin, with broad shoulders, and best of all, his straight pearly white teeth. His smile was everything plus he had style. He was wearing black Levi jeans, fresh white Lacoste tennis shoes and a black leather jacket with a fresh white t-shirt underneath his nice deep waves in his hair. He was gorgeous but I wasn't going to act like no groupie, but the way I was looking at him he knew he had me. I didn't mind at all because I knew I had him by the way he was staring at me like he wanted to eat me for dessert. I had my hair in a middle part straightened and long, my royal blue ballerina looking dress, tanned open toe heels, gold draped earrings with gold bracelets to match on both arms, and my gold chain flowing between my breasts, which were standing at attention and clearly had his. Cora and the crew called me letting me

24

know they were ready to head outside, so Drew yelled back to them "Don't worry; your friend is in good hands." Cora gave me that look and I gave her the nod that everything was cool. Drew walked with me outside of the club and then asked me for my number. I was hesitant as my first reaction is to make up a lie about already having a man when any guy asks me for my number, but there was something different about Drew that peaked my curiosity. "How about you give me your number and I might call you later," I said flirtingly. "So you want to play hard to get? Ok, I like that. I like to work for what I want," he replied. I bit my lip as I stored his number in my phone he then walked me over go to my friends. As I was trying to leave, he held on to my hand and said "Are you sure you want to leave me?" The sound of his voice was so sexy- it was deep but smooth and those lips, those oh so kissable lips. I smiled and went in the car. He shut my door and told Leena "Make sure the lovely Bonnie calls me." Leena laughed and said "Oh I will cause she needs some dick!" We all laughed and Jayna drove off so we could find somewhere to go eat. I watched Drew staring at me until I was out of sight from the rear view mirror. We went through the drive thru at McDonald's and headed home.

As soon as I got home I stripped off my clothes and hopped in my queen sized bed tempted to call Drew, but I decided to let him wait and fell asleep. A week later, after listening to my girls go on and on about how cute Drew is and how I should call him, I decided to do so. A girl picked up and I felt my heart fall all the way to my ass. I didn't even ask for Drew, I just hung up. About ten minutes later I saw Drew's number on my phone. I answered, "Hello?" He asked, "Bonnie, is that you?" "Yes!" I said with an attitude. "Why do you sound upset lovely?" I smiled but I stayed firm, "Because I called you and a woman, I assume your girlfriend, answered your phone. I'm not about the games Drew so just forget I called and erase my number." He responded quickly almost cutting me off, "Wait

25

a minute, girlfriend? What girlfriend? I'm single and if I had a girl I wouldn't have approached you. I may look like a player but that's not my style." I was so happy to hear him say that but I still had to ask, "So who was the girl that answered your phone?" "That was my older sister. I was putting her bags in the cab because she's leaving for New York. She's studying at NYU to become a fashion designer." "Oh," I said feeling a bit stupid for copping an attitude with him before, but I would rather be safe than sorry and not waste my time with someone else's man. "You thought I had a girlfriend?" He started laughing and said, "How cute, we're not even dating yet and you're already getting jealous." "I'm not jealous you nerd, I'm just not a side chick," I replied. "I know you're not a side chick. You're to fly to be a side chick. In due time, you'll be my chick, my one and only." Drew rapped his affection for me. "I can only date one at a time as it doesn't seem easy juggling 2 different girls at once. That's not how I was raised anyway." Those words meant everything to me. To even think that such a man existed that didn't think that getting in every girls' panties was the sole goal, made me want to get to know Drew better. After our conversation that afternoon, Drew and I talked every day and became closer as time went on, which was new to me. Everyone knew I never gave guys the time of day, but Drew was different. However, no matter how different he was, I still had to make him wait awhile until I knew I wanted him to be the one to take my virginity.

My girls started noticing a change in me. I was glowing with happiness and walking around with a stupid smile on my face. The more Drew and I grew closer, I started to spend less time with my friends; some of them understood, as I was just getting into a relationship, but there was one that didn't like it too much - Hazel. She was pregnant and miserable, and misery loves company. Hazel was now reaping what she sewed. She was pregnant, alone, feeling trapped and undesirable as she couldn't keep up with all of her usual scheming, and she finally started to realize that everything I told her was coming to pass. Leon was controlling her; where she went, how she dressed and even what she ate. It was sad to see but what could I say except I told her so. She thought having a baby would make him change his ways, but we all know you can't turn a hoe into a trophy, and Leon and Hazel's situation was living proof. Leon was still sleeping around with other girls, going out partying every night and drinking, instead of getting his act together and preparing for life with his child on the way. He didn't go with her to any of the doctor appointments to ensure that their baby was growing healthy, I did. Sometimes I felt like I was the father of her child the way I was always there for Hazel on demand whenever she needed me.

Once Hazel noticed that someone else was taking up my time she started to get envious. She rolled her eyes when I gushed about Drew to the girls or if I told them stories about the things we did or the stuff he bought me. Everyone was supportive of my new, growing relationship except for Hazel, but I didn't care. I was falling for Drew more and more each day, and as the summer was coming to an end and I was entering my last year at Kingston, I wanted to make sure I spent as much time on my relationship as I could if I wanted to make it last through a stressful and busy year applying for Colleges and Universities. Drew was what I wanted. Someone with morals, respect for women and I love that he was so close with his mom. I adored him for that and he adored me. After about a month and a half we started fooling around - foreplay, kissing, and dry sex. I wasn't ready to give it up to him yet. I wanted him to wait a little longer before I gave him someone I couldn't get back. I liked him a lot but I wanted to be in love with the person I gave myself too. I've never been in love before but I felt like I could fall in love with Drew. My mother liked him, my little sisters loved him and my dad wasn't too fond of me dating, but I was turning 18 in a few months and my dad knew I had my head on straight and wouldn't do anything I wasn't sure of or pressured into, so he was cool with me seeing Drew. But although I was trust worthy, I sometimes felt that I couldn't trust myself around Drew. He was sweet, gentle and willing to wait for me. A lot of guys wouldn't wait, no matter how fine you are but I could tell Drew wasn't just in it to hit it. I know he wanted to badly, but the more and more we got to know each other, he really got to know me for who I really am. He told me how much he loved my mind, he's mentioned plenty of times that he admired my body but he cherished my heart. We had numerous deep conversations; the way he stimulates my mind made him more alluring to me. He graduated a year ago and was going to start college early the following year. I admired the fact that he had his head on straight and goals he set out to attain. Don't get me wrong, he liked to party and have fun but he made sure he took care of what was more important first. Drew wanted to be a Pediatrician because he loved kids and got along with them so well; my little sisters loved when he came over, he played with them before he even gave me attention but I was cool with it because it was sweet. Oddly enough, it comforted me a bit to think that he would make a great dad if we had kids one day, but I'm not trying to get ahead of myself. Drew and I talked about everything, our aspirations, life struggles, experiences, family and friends. He even talked about his first love, a girl named Gina. Some Arabic girl he used to go to school with. They were serious. They dated for about 2 years and they lost their virginity to each other. It made me feel like I had competition, but Drew knew me so well, so he reassured me that she's not a recurring girl in his life because she cheated on him with someone on the football team. He wasn't down for that so he broke up with her and they never got back together. I asked him if she ever tried to get back with him and he told me flat out, "A few times, but even though I still cared for her at the time I knew I couldn't trust her. Once a cheater, always a cheater. Whenever we bump into each other she always tells me how she wishes things were different but I know better. Plus, my mom hates her and I wouldn't date a woman my mother doesn't approve of, but you don't have to worry about that baby girl, Mama D likes you and that's all I need to know." Hearing that made my day. Drew and I talked what seemed like twenty times a day, and we sent each other lovey dovey text messages all day long - I never went to bed without talking to him.

But I noticed the more time we spent together, the more Hazel got jealous. She would make rude comments like "It's always sweet in the beginning," or "It's not going last, there's something I don't like about him." Even Cora and Leena began to see her jealousy, but I just ignored her and played it off as she was just annoyed that she was no longer the center of attention. She was just mad that she never had what I had. While Hazel stayed worried about Leon's every move, I knew where my man was. She hated when I was on the phone with him around her, so much that she would always leave the room. I felt that she should have been happy for me, especially since I never had a serious boyfriend. It was a bit annoying that the first time I had someone I really liked and who made me happy, someone I would have loved telling my best friend about, all she kept doing was hating on my relationship. It made me question our friendship. I'm always there for Hazel, even when she's wrong, but now when I wanted her to be happy for me, she kept making up all kind of reasons to not like Drew when there wasn't even one reason why she shouldn't. I tried not to say anything about it, because she was already stressed out about Leon and I didn't want to put any stress on the baby. I told myself that is was the pregnancy hormones and she would get over whatever it is that she was going through, but as summer flew by she became more and more jealous.

Fall had arrived and although school was back in session, I was still living in bliss, due to my romance with Drew, that I had barely noticed. Over 4 months, I had become close with Drew's family and he also introduced me to all of his friends. We planned to take a trip to New York City to visit his sister in the summer after I graduated, as she was going to school for fashion and Drew knew I was interested in working in the same field. He always says, "Rihanna ain't got anything on you babe!" He loved making me smile and I adored him for that.

November was approaching and Drew's birthday was coming up. I didn't know what to get him but I had something in mind. Drew and I had been going strong for five months and we were getting really serious, so I wanted to plan something romantic and intimate for just the two of us. I made reservations at the Hilton Hotel overlooking the Falls for the weekend, and reserved a private table for two with champagne and candlelight at the Brasa Brazilian Steakhouse - The night before Drew and I went to Niagara Falls to celebrate his birthday, I met up with the girls for dinner at Turtle Jack's to have a little girl talk and let them know my plans for Drew's birthday. Jenelle was the first to make a comment and burst out "Girl, it's about time you gave it up to someone!" Cora smiled and said, "Now that sounds like a night to remember!" The girls thought it was a good idea, all except Hazel of course. "Out of all the people that tried to holla at you, you want to give it up to Drew after just a few months? You better hope he doesn't break your heart after he gets the kitty." Leena interrupted Hazel, "Drew is a good guy. He has a lot going for him and he treats her well. Why wouldn't she give it up to him? If you asked me, he deserves it." I rolled my eyes at Hazel and tried not to let her rain on my parade. As we were eating this girl walked up to me and asked "Are you Drew's girl?" I replied "Yes, and who's asking?" She gave me attitude and said, "Obviously I am. No need to be rude, I just wanted to introduce myself. My name is Gina, Drew's first love. He must have told you about me." Hazel sat up with a smirk on her face. "Oh, yes. Drew mentioned you briefly once. You're the ex that fucked someone else while you were dating Drew," I answered Gina calmly with a grin. My girls burst out laughing and you could tell Gina was so embarrassed, as she clearly wasn't expecting me to say that. "Well I hope he treats you better than he treats his other girls," she responded. "Jayna got up and started telling her off, "Maybe if you focused on keeping your legs closed, you would be able to hold down a man like my girl. Seems to me you're just mad that someone else has what you use to have and clearly still want. Now remove yourself of our table before force needs to be used." Gina walked off with her friend and left. "I told you he can't be trusted," Hazel exclaimed. "How can he not be trusted when he told me everything? He's clearly not still into her or she would be throwing that in my face. Not every guy is like Leon, Hazel." "I can't believe you would say that to me Bonnie, I'm pregnant and going through a bunch of shit. Ever since you got this new boyfriend, you've changed, acting all brand new on your girls." My blood started to boil, I couldn't take her smart ass comments anymore, I just had to say something. "I've changed? I'm acting brand new? Are you serious Hazel?! I might spend a lot of time with Drew but I still find time for my friends. This is my first serious relationship and instead of you being happy for me, you belittle it and assume the worse about Drew instead of getting to know him. Everyone else is supportive but you! I would prefer that you keep your rude remarks to yourself since you never have anything nice to say." She was shocked. I never told Hazel off before and she clearly wasn't having it so she stormed off and left. At that moment, I didn't even care about her feelings and she clearly didn't care about mine. After that night, Hazel and I didn't speak for a couple of weeks. I didn't want Hazel's negative thoughts messing with my decision to make love to Drew.

After weeks of planning for Drew's birthday it was finally here. I was so nervous and excited, I didn't bother to tell him I saw his ex the night before, and I didn't give my words with Hazel a second thought. Drew and I left for the Falls around 6'oclock to celebrate his 19th birthday. I wore my hair in a high top bun, gold chandelier earrings, a baby doll light pink dress, some orange strappy heels and no underwear. Drew wore dark blue denim jeans, a white button up dress shirt and stylish dress shoes that I got him from Aldo. On our drive to the Falls he had his right hand on my left thigh and his left hand on the wheel. I slid his hand up my dress so he could feel what he was about to get into. I could tell he was getting excited by the sudden bulge in his jeans. We pulled up to the restaurant and as soon as I got out the car Drew grabbed me and kissed me passionately and said "I love you." I looked deep into his eyes and replied "I love you." He placed his hands on my ass and gripped it as we made out. I could tell he wanted me bad and I wanted him just as much. When we finally got our hands off each other, we headed into the restaurant and ordered some wine to get our night started. Drew ordered for me- he became a master at knowing what I liked. Most girls would have felt that their independence was being taken away but I enjoy a man who knew when to take charge. Our waiter was a young woman who seemed to have a crush on Drew which we could both tell by the way she kept coming over to ask him if he needed anything, but he always said something clever to her even after he told her, "No thank you, my baby and I are good," but the bitch just didn't get the point, but I didn't even care because Drew was mine. We laughed and talked throughout dinner while we sipped on wine and took a few shots of Vodka. I could tell he was having a good time and so was I. After a few drinks, we were feeling nice. We walked over to the Falls for a romantic stroll holding hands and joking around about the freaky lingerie he saw in my bag. "So the inner freak is coming out tonight, huh? He laughed. "I don't know what you're talking about," I said with a smirk. I felt so warm and secure in his arms, I knew I was making the right decision choosing Drew to be my first. I was so happy and felt so lucky to have found someone that understood me and made me feel special, someone I could truly connect with on all levels. We then headed back to the car to check into our hotel. We made out some more in the elevator as we headed up to the 52nd floor with a premium view of the Falls. Drew picked me up by my ass and I wrapped my legs around him and started grinding on him slowly. He slid his finger up my pussy and felt that I was ready inside. When we exited the elevator Drew was still carrying me and put me down after we walked into our room. I had requested rose peddles on the bed with scented vanilla candles. He looked at me and gave me a kiss on my forehead. He walked over to the window to admire the view while I popped open a bottle of pink Moet. "Happy birthday baby!" We toasted and drank some more. He then said, "Why didn't you tell me you had words with Gina yesterday?" "I didn't think it mattered, it was petty and I didn't feel the need to bring her up... Wait a minute, how do you know what happened?" "She called me a few times and once she realized I wasn't going to answer her calls, she left me a message. I listened and deleted it and thought I would wait for you to mention something," he said. "Sorry babe. I guess I should have told you. Are you mad?" "Of course I'm not mad over you cursing that chick, I'm glad. Maybe she will finally realize how happy I am and stop calling me. But now that we got that out of the way, I just want to say thank you for a great birthday baby girl." I smiled and told him to get comfortable while I took my bag into the washroom to freshen up. He laid on the bed and ordered a movie off of the Pay Per View channel. I took my hair down and put on my black laced lingerie. I sprayed some perfume on the back of my neck, wrist and inner thighs and put on my 6 inch heels. When I came out of the washroom I turned played some music getting Drews attention already in his birthday suit. I was nervous on the inside but refused to make a fool of myself. As the song played, I rolled my waist line slowly to the beat of the song. I then crawled over to the bed and gave Drew a lap dance. He was hard as a rock and built like a stallion. I stood between his legs and kissed him slowly and bit his bottom lip. He slapped my ass so hard, but the sexual tension turned the pain into pleasure. I turned around and started to move each ass cheek to the beat. He couldn't keep his hands off of me. The way I was turning him on was turning me on. I pushed him to lay down on the bed and started to crawl on top of him, licking his defined six pack as I worked my way up to his chest, I bit his right nipple and then began to bite his neck. He was so surprised he said, "Damn baby, you sure you're a virgin? You seem to know what you're doing." I smiled while ignoring his sarcasm and continued doing my thing, until he couldn't take me taking control any longer. He flipped me on by back and threw himself on top of me and began to bite my neck and suck on my tities, kissing my flat stomach, and then made his way down to my pussy. He started to play with my clit as he bit softly on the lips of my pussy. I moaned uncontrollably and grabbed his head; you would swear the boy was a fish the way he didn't come up for air. When he was done pleasing me he made his way up to my lips sucking on my bottom lip. I asked him how my pussy tasted, and he said "Like strawberries." I giggled as he took a quick second to put a condom on slowly spreading my legs as he pushed the tip of his penis in slowly. It hurt but I am a big girl. As I became wetter, he moved a little faster and deeper with each thrust. I felt his penis deep inside of me and I loved it as I loved. Drew took his time with my body and made love to me like I never could have imagined. I enjoyed it and I could tell he enjoyed it too by the way he was moaning while he held my waist line and caressed my neck. I told him it was his and so was I. As he came inside me he then laid on my breasts until we both fell asleep in each other's embrace.

CHAPTER 5: FRIEND OR FOE

After our perfect weekend getaway to celebrate Drew's birthday, of course I called my girls to tell them all about it, especially about my first time. I called Cora who then called Leena and she called the Twins. I explained to my girls that I would call Hazel later to fill her in after we worked out our issues, and they understood. The girls were eager to know what happened with Drew and were asking all types of questions; "How did it go?" "Was he good?" and "How big is he?" I began to tell them how he made my body feel weak in the most pleasurable way, and the freaky things we did. I got as detailed as possible so they could understand what a great lover my man is. Jayna even said, "Seems like Drew was worth the wait." Cora was so happy for me and jokingly said, "Now I'm the only one left in the virgin crew." I laughed and told her that she's next. Jenelle asked if Drew had any friends because she had not been sexed right in months, I chuckled and told her I would ask. "That sounds like some good dick to me," exclaimed Leena and I couldn't argue with that. I was glad my friends were happy for me.

After my phone conference with the girls I got dressed with the intention of heading over to Hazel's house, but as I was walking out the door, Hazel pulled up in my drive-way and beat me to it. I was shocked because usually if anyone of us had an issue with Hazel, we would be the one to extend the olive branch first in an attempt to mend our friendship with her. Hazel never took it upon herself to clear the air first. I stood on my porch and waited for her to walk up to me. "How have you been?" I asked to feel her out. "Alright, I guess," Hazel responded as she shrugged her shoulders and looked off to the side. She then muttered "Can we sit and talk?" I said yes without hesitation as this was already my intention. "I'm sorry for the way I've been acting so negatively towards your relationship with Drew. I know you really like him and he likes you, it's just... I feel all alone, and during this time I need you the most and I feel like I was losing you as my friend. I know you have a separate life outside of us now, I guess I just haven't accepted it yet," Hazel expressed. "I know I spend more time with Drew, but our relationship is new and we're still trying to get to know each other. I'm not trying to put anybody on the back burner but this is normal for girls to do. You and Leena have both done it too. It's just new for you to experience because I have never been in a relationship before so I was available twenty-four-seven for everyone else's relationship issues because I had none of my own." As I explained my feelings to Hazel, she smiled and we embraced each other like old friends who were back on track. I was so happy she was trying to be understanding and not make this about her as she always did. I hated fighting with Hazel, she was my best friend. I still couldn't help but feel a little uneasy about trusting her completely though. It wasn't that I didn't want to, but I just had a gut feeling that I shouldn't. Hazel's phone rang, which she looked at and then pressed ignore. Something seemed very odd because Hazel always answered her phone in front of me, she didn't have any reason not to. I knew her deepest darkest secrets so I had to ask, "Who was that?" She replied, "My mom. She's just calling to see if I'm ok. Leon and I broke up again." I wasn't surprised but I still asked her what happened. She said she found a girl's thong in his room at the side of his bed. I shook my head as she continued "We have been having so many problems lately and I'm sick of it all. I'm having our baby boy in a few months and I still have to go to the doctor's office because he keeps giving me S.T.D.'s. I then responded sounding irritated, "You shouldn't be fucking him unless he's wearing a damn condom," although I really wanted to say that she shouldn't be sleeping with his nasty ass at all! As she finished talking to me about her baby daddy problems, she then asked me how Drew's birthday went. I was happy that she asked because I really wanted to tell my best friend about my first time. As I started to tell her, she really got into it as Hazel is a very sexual girl. She loved her sex stories and to finally hear mine made it even better. I got into as much explicit details and watched her eyes light up with excitement and a little envy. I think after hearing the story she might have grown a crush on Drew or had thoughts of screwing him, but she wouldn't be that stupid to cross that line because as much as we were best friends, I would still beat that ass. Don't get it confused, I would never fight over a guy, but in that scenario, it would come down to the principle. We chilled some more and talked about her and Donna's blooming friendship. They seemed to be growing closer again and making future play dates for their kids, which was good to hear because my mom was having a dinner the day after Christmas to celebrate the holiday and I wanted my whole crew to be there to get to know Drew better. As we continued to talk, her phone rang about five more times and she ignored each call, which made me think that Hazel was up to no good. I don't know if she was fucking someone else's man or planning to rob a bank, but I felt like something was off with her. Maybe I was making something out of nothing, but my gut has yet to misguide me. I guess only time will tell. After awhile of chilling and catching up, Hazel decided to go home to get some rest. As I watched her walk to her car, I saw her pull out her phone and it appeared as though she was calling back her mystery caller whom she kept ignoring. As she was getting into her car and talking on the phone, she had a sneaky looking grin on her face. I went inside after she drove off trying to ignore my unsettling feelings.

The next day Drew and I met up for lunch at PHO's as they served the best Vietnamese food and then went back to his

38

place. We fooled around and had a quickie before his mother came home. He had to do some laundry after what my body fluids did to his sheets. He proceeded to the basement to start a load of laundry while I remained upstairs in his room putting my clothes back on. I heard a beep over on his night table so I picked up his phone to see who it is. "I'm glad we got around to having a talk yesterday. It's good to know you don't hate me. Maybe we can meet up again soon and have an "innocent" good time" with an inserted smiley face - a message from his ex-Gina. I was so furious that I slammed his phone back down and starting rushing to get my clothes on so I could get out of there. Drew came back upstairs, "Do you want something to drink baby?" I looked at him and kissed my teeth. "What did I do?" Drew asked. He instantly knew I was upset with him. "Check your phone," I said as I tried to walk past him to leave. He held my arm so I couldn't leave before he knew what I so mad about and picked up his phone to look at the most recent text message. He let out a big sigh while rolling his eyes. The look I gave him showed him that he had about two seconds to explain himself immediately. "She called me from a different number; she completely caught me off guard. I asked her what she wanted and she said closure. She went on saying how she was sorry for cheating on me and not being a woman about it, and how she didn't want me to hate her. I told her that I didn't hate her but that I would rather keep our communication at the bare minimum if we ran into each other because I don't need any problems. She said ok, that's fine and asked if we could work on our friendship. I told her that I would prefer my space so that you and I could be together and that we are happy. I jokingly said that maybe one day we could go to lunch but not now. She laughed and we ended things on a good note. Drew thought that his explanation would fix the misunderstanding, but personally, I didn't like it. I felt like Gina was up to something. Although I believed him, I still gave him the cold shoulder as I was still a bit upset. Drew was never ok with that, he always did something to make me smile or to take my mind off the subject, he hated seeing me mad or sad. I know he valued our relationship and wouldn't want to do anything to destroy it. He started kissing me all over my face and began to kiss my neck- knowing that was my weak spot. I laughed and moaned and felt on his dick and before I knew it, we were back to having our clothes off. This was our first go at make-up sex and it was good. It made me brush off my anger from reading the message from his ex, but I knew in the back of my mind that she was up to no good.

My mother's Christmas party was the following weekend and she asked me to help her cook and get things for the party. We had a large family and a lot of friends coming and she wanted everything to be perfect. We cooked fried chicken, oxtail, rice and peas, fish, lasagna, macaroni pie, garlic shrimp, steak and pasta salad. My mom was known her cooking and I learned from the best of course. We had enough liquor to give each person alcohol poisoning, twice. The week flew by fast and the day of the party had finally arrived. Our guests started to roll in one after the other. My mother's best friend Juju, dad's college friends, our cousins, aunts and uncles on both sides, and my grandparents. Then I had my people; Pay, Dready, Coolie boy and my girls came through looking like fashionista and dapper men. Even Donna and Hazel pulled off some stylish outfits to complement their pregnant glow. As the party got going the drinks kept pouring. Everybody was having a good time. I introduced Drew to Pay, Deadly and Coolie boy - Coolie boy always had a crush on me so he wasn't too keen on meeting Drew. He even pulled me over to a corner and said "You can do better, and by better, I mean me." I laughed and gave him a kiss on the cheek to shut him up. I even noticed Hazel getting to know Drew a bit which is exactly what I hoped for, so she could see what a great guy he is. I went to the kitchen to help my mother dish out food for everyone, and noticed Drew and Hazel had disappeared from our spot where our crew was chilling. I went looking for them instantly. It's not that I didn't trust Drew, it was more that I didn't trust Hazel. When I got upstairs to look in my room, I saw Drew laying on my bed, it looked like he drank too much. I gave him a kiss on his forehead and told him I would be back. As I was walking down the stairs I heard Hazel's voice coming from the washroom. "Hey Gigi, I'm still here at the party... Ya, he's here too..." The conversation sounded very fishy. Hazel and I knew each other's friends and out of the seven years I've known her, I've never heard her mention anyone by the name "Gigi" before. I was steady trying to find out who she was talking to. She had mentioned to whoever it was on the phone that she couldn't talk right now and would call them back after the party. I quickly left to go back to the party so I didn't get caught ease dropping. When Hazel came out of the washroom, she sat beside me and asked me how I was, "I'm good. Everything ok with you?" I asked. "Just good," she replied with a smile on her face. After a night of laughter, fun and games, it got really late so our guests started to leave. I made Drew stay because he was really drunk. I had to convince my dad to let Drew stay in the guest room. I walked my friends out and watched them get in their cabs. I didn't see Hazel so I went to look for her. She was at the side of my house on the phone again. She was talking to the person named "Gigi" again, "I'm leaving right now. No, I don't think she knows." I interrupted her by asking what she was doing. "You startled me," she said as she told the person on the phone she had to go and hung up. I looked at her weird and she gave me a fake smile. "I'm going to Leon's to talk. I'll call you tomorrow," she said as she walked to her car. I went inside with only one thing on my mind - Hazel acting shady. Now all I needed to figure out was who it was towards this time around.

CHAPTER 6: CHEERS

New Year's Eve was here and I had decided to ring in the New Year with Drew instead of the girls. They understood and no one made a big fuss about it, not even Hazel. Drew and I planned to stay at my house since my parents and sisters weren't going to be home. I planned a nice romantic dinner for the two of us and Drew was going to rent some movies for our night in. He came over with snacks, a bottle of vodka and pink Moet- which he knew was my favorite- and his overnight bag. He came inside and put the stuff down on the table in the foyer of my house, walked over to me and put the mistletoe over our heads and said "Give me a kiss ma." I placed myself on my tippy toes to give him a kiss and he grabbed my ass to bring me closer. Drew then went into the living room and yelled, "What movie do you want to watch babe? The Orphan or The Hills Have Eyes?" "That's all you got? You know I hate scary movies," I complained as I fixed our plates. "Don't worry lovely, you can hide your beautiful face in my muscular chest." He laughed as I gave him a stank look with a slight smirk on my face. I brought our plates into the living room and poured a glass of Moet for the both of us. I sat down beside him as we ate dinner and watched the Orphan. As soon as we were done eating I noticed it was 11:57 p.m. I poured us another glass of Moet and ran to the kitchen for the chocolate covered strawberries and whipped cream. "Cheers baby! I look forward to many more years together," he said while leaning in to kiss me at 12:00 o'clock on the dot. I then took his glass and mine, and placed them down. I climbed on top of him slowly and started to kiss his lips passionately while I took off his shirt and unbuckled his jeans. Using the whipped cream, I drew a rose on his chest with the stem leading down to the tip of his erection. I started licking the whipped cream off of his chest moving my tongue slowly down his shaft. He grabbed my hair once I took his well-groomed manhood straight into my mouth sucking in fast motion, I didn't let him ease his way into it, I went straight for it and about 1 minute later, I started licking and just sucking on the tip. Drew couldn't take it anymore; he ripped off my dress and put that mother-fucker in without hesitation while letting out a quiet moan of increased satisfaction. He placed both of his hands on my firm cheeks and moved my ass in the motion he wanted me to go. He used his teeth to lightly pull on my nipple ring. I tightened my pussy going down on his dick which led him to moan and bite my shoulder. I began to ride him fast and slow with the movie playing in the background. He turned me around to hit it from the back slapping my firmness as he came inside of me. We sexed our way well into the New Year, going rounds in every place in my house. He propped my legs up and sat me on the table making me his dessert in the kitchen; he put me in the wheelbarrow position with the help of my living room stairs; and, we played around as he was chasing me naked all around the house. We couldn't keep our hands off of each other, between his sex drive and mine, we could go all night and find different ways to please each other.

After all the fun and games, we took a shower together and laid in my bed naked and talked as he stroked his fingers through my hair. "Imagine if you never took my number, we wouldn't be doing this right now," he said. "I'm so glad I did," I responded with a smile on my face. I told him I love him and he then placed a gentle kiss on my forehead and got up and went into his bag. He pulled out a rectangular box with a red ribbon neatly tied around it keeping its contents hidden. He climbed back into my bed handing me the box saying, "This is just one of the ways I wanted to let you know how much you mean to me." I pulled the ends of the string to reveal a beautiful heart necklace. I sat up and watched him in the mirror as he put the necklace around my neck. I told him, "I have a surprise for you too," handed him a whip and handcuffs and teased, "You know what to do with them, right?" After thanking each other for a wonderful evening, we cuddled and fell asleep in each other's arms.

CHAPTER 7: ROUND AND ROUND

Leena White was a wild one. She was rebellious towards her parents and fearless facing any situation; she even told Hazel straight up that she was fucked up for sleeping with Pay. She was never about hiding how she feels. Not even regarding her personal life. She would tell people if she had a yeast infection or when she was on her period. She was bold when it came to putting her business out there; but, as much as Leena was quick to voice her opinion she was naive towards her own situation. Leena has been dating a guy name Rayon. He was a cutie with dreads but a bad boy to the core. He was known for flirting with girls and breaking the law, but he also has a more serious issue - his heavy use of Molly. His parents were successful, rich and provided everything Rayon wanted. One night when he was in college Rayon was at a party in Castlemore and was introduced to the party goers' drug of choice, Molly. He tried it with his older cousin for the first time and was hooked. Since then, that became Rayon's energy booster. When he was on it, he was a completely different person and developed an entirely different attitude than when he was sober; he was wild, belligerent, passive aggressive he broke into cars and houses, and he even robbed a cabman before. Other than his erratic behavior when he was under the influence of Molly, when he was sober he was loving, compassionate, sweet and funny - those were the qualities Leena fell in love with Rayon for, but things changed. Rayon didn't just start acting crazy and disrespectful, he also started hitting Leena. I think we all saw Rayon hit Leena at least once, when we were at Pay's house party. Everybody was in the living room and when I got up to go to the washroom, I saw Rayon and Leena in the guest room and he back-handed her

45

across her face. I was about to say something and Leena ran towards me and locked the both of us in the main washroom. "Please Bonnie, I know you care but please… Just let it go." I agreed, as Leena begged me with a desperate look in her eyes. There was another incident that occurred which also should have been Leena's big hint to leave Rayon, when he was high on Molly again and started to feel on Jenelle's breasts when she was sleeping over at Leena's one night. Jenelle woke up out of her sleep to see Rayon feeling on her and she pushed him off and told him to fuck off. He smiled at her like a creep and said nothing, just walked away. Jenelle told Leena the next day but Leena refused to believe her. She called Jenelle all type of names and didn't speak to her for weeks. From that point forward, we all knew that Leena would not leave Rayon no matter what he did, so we decided to keep his shadiness to ourselves.

The final test of Leena's patience and naiveté was a despicable one. One day in August of this year, Rayon called Leena and said he was going to take her to the movies. An hour had past and Rayon still hadn't come to pick up Leena. She waited until 11:30 p.m., four hours later, and then realized he wasn't coming. This wasn't the first time he had done something like this. Leena called him repeatedly and got no response. She had an idea where he was, so she decided to take it upon herself to find him and confront him about standing her up. When Leena arrived at Rayon's cousin's house, she went to the back and peeped through the living room window only to see Rayon eating out some girl on the living room floor. There were cocaine lines, pills and shot glasses on the table, so she knew Rayon was using heavily. She was furious, she got all dressed up only to be stood up and then find her man cheating on her. Leena banged on the back door startling Rayon and the random girl he was having for dinner. The girl put on her pants as Rayon went to answer the door. "What?" He said to Leena like she was the one giving another girl pleasure. "What? That's all you have to say?" She kicked him in his balls and slapped him across his face with her clutch. Rayon fell to the ground and Leena walked off. Once Leena got in her car, Rayon ran up to the vehicle and punched the glass, slightly cracking it. Leena scream and tried to put the key in the ignition, but she didn't realize that the door was unlocked. Rayon opened the car door and pulled Leena out by her hair. He slapped her in the face multiple times, kicking her to the ground then standing her back up so he could kick her down again. Rayon just kept hitting her, until his cousin ran out to intervene. I don't want to even imagine what could have resulted if his cousin didn't come out to stop Rayon. Leena scrapped herself off the bloody pavement and managed to get inside of her car and drove home. She walked with a limp inside her house and went straight upstairs to her bedroom to avoid her parents. She looked at herself in the mirror and saw the damage Rayon had done to her. She looked at herself in disappointment and removed herself from the mirror. She took off her clothes to take a bath and could only feel the tenderness of her rib cage. Leena lit her candles and played music. As she lay in the bathtub she reflected on the beating that was inflicted on her by Rayon, someone she loved, and began to cry some more. When she came out to get ready for bed, she noticed that she had missed two calls from Rayon. As she sat on her bed in her towel, she debated if she should call him back. It wasn't too long before she gave into temptation as soon as Rayon called for a third time. "What do you want, Rayon?" she said with a blast of attitude and sadness in her voice. "I want to talk, can you come outside." Leena walked over to her window to see Rayon waving to her with an innocent smirk on his face. She told him she was coming and hung up the phone. Leena threw on some clothes and went outside to meet Rayon. As soon as she closed her door Rayon grabbed Leena and started to kiss her. "Get the fuck off me! Are you crazy?! You beat me like a man and then think that kissing me is going to make it better? You can't be that stupid." Leena was perplexed. "I'm ashamed of what I did and sorry will never fix it. I was high out of my mind, I don't know what I was thinking," Rayon replied. "You need help Ray. I can't do this anymore. I don't want to have to explain where I got these bruises from. It's embarrassing," Leena said softly, hoping he would understand how badly this was affecting her. "I'll get help baby, I promise," Rayon replied trying to put her mind at ease and reel her back in. As much as Leena wanted to believe him, she knew better, but knowing the truth still didn't stop her from hoping he would change. Rayon held her closer, embracing her bruised body and whispered slowly in her ear, "I need you" Those words made Leena melt and suckered her in. "It's really important that you try to change Ray. I'm not always going to be here." As much as Leena sounded serious Rayon knew she wasn't going anywhere. He just had to come up with some new ways to manipulate her. Rayon kissed her to shut her up. She showed him in and led him upstairs to her room. "Put on a movie, we can have our movie night right now," Rayon said as he sat on her bed. She put in Transformers 3 and went to sit next to Rayon. Not even five minutes into the movie and Rayon started kissing on Leena's neck, touching her thigh and moving his hands on the side of her stomach. "Ouch!" Leena said as he touched the bruised rib he caused. "Sorry baby." He started to kiss alongside her ribs. Rayon went on top of her, kissing her bruised body; he then began to kiss her kitty kat, he knew that was Leena's weak spot. She then returned the favor and Rayon sat back and enjoyed it. Leena was given many compliments on her head game. When they finished their make-up sex sensation, Rayon and Leena cuddled up for the rest of the night. Rayon woke up at four o'clock so he could leave before it was time for her parents to go to work. "I love you," Rayon said. "I love you too," Leena replied. Rayon left and Leena went back to bed thinking about a lie to tell everyone when they saw the fresh bruises knowing there was probably more to come.

CHAPTER 8: REAL TO THE CORE/A

Cora was a lovely girl and a great friend. She was supportive of anything her friends and family aspired to be. She was one of those people who believed in your dream as much as you would. She kept it real about everything. For example, if she didn't like your outfit she would tell you, but in a way that you would both laugh about it. Cora is one of the good ones. She has big dreams and goals she intends to achieve, she's beautiful, sweet and knows how to have fun. If a fight broke out at a club she would always be the peace-marker. She wasn't like some of us in the crew, always ready to fight, she just wanted to go out and have a good time. She was stylish and smart, someone who always has a great vibe to be around. Cora was an only child, raised by her dad due to her mother passing away while giving birth to her sister, which also led to the baby's death. That was a hard time for Cora but her belief in God gave her faith to get through it, and she continues to look at the situation in a positive way. Like she always says, "Everything happens for a reason. I might not understand it now, but one day I will all in good timing." I loved her way of thinking. We have a lot of similarities; we're spiritual, have big dreams and look at life in a positive way. With the way Hazel's been acting shady lately, Cora and I started to chill more.

Cora and I decided to go and visit Donna and her baby girl, Nelly once she returned home from the hospital and settled in. She was as cute as a button. She had Donna's green eyes, light skin with little curly hair. As we entered the grand lobby of Donna's mom's condo, Cora and I saw Pay getting into a car. We went upstairs and knocked on Donna's door. "Hi girlies! I missed you guys!" Donna said with a big smile on her face. We hugged, and then Cora and I entered into the kitchen to wash our hands to hold baby Nelly. "What's been going on with you Donna? How's motherhood treating you?" Cora asked. "It's good. It keeps me super busy, but Nelly is a good baby. She sleeps through the majority of the night and she's always smiling which keeps a smile on my face. Those are the things that make the hard times worth it, you know?!" Donna replied. "That's good to hear doll. How's Pay handling baby daddy duties?" I asked. "He sucks at it! Well, just when it comes to responsibilities like, changing diapers, bathing her or feeding her in the middle of the night. But he does take her out and spoils her with a lot of toys and clothes. Nelly doesn't go without anything, but I feel he believes that contributes so much in the financial department that he doesn't have to do the hard stuff. He's always gone, partying just as much and comes home late… It's like I take care of the baby by myself. I always have to ask him for money and I hate it. I need to find a job but then I'm going to have to pay for a babysitter, and how would I continue school then? I really didn't think it would be like this." As Donna vented you could hear the frustration in her voice. Nelly was about four months old and Pay hadn't taken on any of the responsibilities. I could tell it was only going to get worse from here. How worse? We would see soon enough. Cora and I felt bad for Donna. "Have you done a budget of how much money you would need and have to spend in a month for you and Nelly?", I asked. "No…" Donna replied. "I don't like the way Pay is treating you in this situation and I want you to be happy. Whenever you're ready to look for a job, let me know and I will help you. We will work on a budget and see what expenses you would have so you will be able to support you and Nelly. Fuck Pay!" Cora said with aggression. Donna and I looked at each other and burst out laughing "Fuck Pay!" Donna and I both chanted. Cora was known to keep it real to the core. We loved her for

51

that. She would fight for her friends no matter what the situation was.

Cora did help Donna prepare a budget and look for employment on their spare time; and, perhaps it was good practice, as Cora was starting college in a few months to major in Business Management. She had many ventures that she wanted to start and she wanted to educate herself as much as possible. She was registered to study at George Brown College located in downtown Toronto. She was focused, which made me want to follow suit once I finished my last year of high school.

A few months into my relationship with Drew, we both decided to introduce Cora to Drew's friend, Trey, who Cora had developed a crush on and Drew informed me that Trey was feeling Cora as well. He was brown skinned, had brown curly hair, and big brown eyes. Some of his people call him "brown boy," not only due to his complexion, hair and physical appearance, but because he had money. He never carried anything less than hundred dollar bills. That dude would go into a dollar store and buy a drink for a dollar and pay for it with a hundred-dollar bill. Drew and Trey had been friends since Grade 1, but he was nothing like Drew. Trey liked fast money, pharmaceutical money. Plus, that was all he knew, it was how he was raised. He comes from a long blood line of drug traffickers, living a life style that a lot of people would wish to have. Cora was a good girl but got herself a bad boy. Trey treated her good though, he was always checking in with her, taking her out and showering her with gifts. He made her feel special. Cora had been talking to Trey for a few months now, but still hasn't given Trey any play; I don't blame her, you have to let these dudes wait a while before they get that 'cookie'. Trey hated that he had to wait but he really adored Cora and wanted more than just sex from her. Cora told me that they would even get into arguments after a little foreplay, because he would get so into it, and try slipping in more than just his fingers. Cora wasn't having it! No matter how much she liked Trey she wasn't going to have no one make her feel pressured into doing anything she might regret. Trey tried to respect that but I guess because he was so accustomed to getting pussy whenever and wherever he wanted, he wasn't expecting to be shut down by Cora; but, this also made him respect her even more. Trey liked the challenge and appreciated that he could trust that Cora wasn't after him for his money, so he didn't want to jeopardize the loyalty she showed him. He loved her realness and her love for life. That kept him from straying and to learn how to become patient, and that's all Cora really needed. Besides their petty arguments, they really cared for one another. One time, Trey came down with the flu and Cora left school just so she could go and take care of him; and another time, when Cora went to Buffalo to go shopping and her Coach Bus left her, he drove all the way there to get her. It was the little things that kept their relationship blossoming into something real. The longer Cora made Trey wait for her, the deeper their relationship became. Cora was falling for Trey more and more every day, but she hated the fact that she always had to worry about him given his line of work. She hated that he sold drugs; she wished so badly that he would give it up and turn his life around. That's the only thing she said she would change about him. But as much as she talked to him about getting out of the game, it was going in one ear and coming out the other. As much as he loved Cora, Trey loved living in the fast lane and no one was going to change that. A few weeks before school started they had a serious break up because she almost got shot during a drive-by in Toronto around Jane and Finch. I've never seen Cora so angry and afraid. I think she was really scared of losing someone again that she really cared about. She only knew how to show her sadness through anger. Cora cursed him out so badly and told him she never wanted to see him again.

He would call for days but she would ignore his calls; that is until he climbed in her window one night and woke her up out of her sleep, "What the fuck are you doing, Trey? Are you fucking crazy?!" Cora yelled. "I'm sorry but we need to talk. I miss you, baby. I know I fucked up but I can't lose you. I need you. I love you," Trey poured his heart out to Cora. "I love you too Trey, but how do you think it makes me feel knowing I could lose you at any time? I don't want to have to go through that. I lost my mom and my baby sister, I don't want to think of losing you too," Cora cried. Trey looked in to her eyes and felt her pain, he understood where she was coming from, as he also lost a few people to the life he chose. "I'm going to try to change, I promise. Just let me stack up my bread some more and I'll get out. You have my word boo," Trey expressed. They kissed each other passionately; both happy to hold each other, love each other, and to be with each other again. They felt their bond strengthened more that night and only wanted it to grow even more with time.

CHAPTER 9: DOUBLE TROUBLE

Jayna and Jenelle were rebellious and wild, and lived everyday like it was their last. We all liked to have a good time, but they took it to another level. When Jayna and Jenelle weren't with us, best believe they weren't sitting home waiting for the next wild party to go to, they went out and made their own fun. They also had a bad reputation because of their careless ways. One time when they were at summer school, a girl named Lisa walked in and heard what sounded like two people having sex, which was really Jayna eating a girl out in the washroom stall. Lisa waited for whoever was in the stall to come out and when Jayna and the girl came out of the stall, Lisa stood there looking at them smirking. As she turned her back to walk out and run her mouth, Jayna grabbed Lisa by her hair, pulled her down to the ground and said, "I dare you to open up your mouth; I bet it will be the last words you speak." Jayna pulled out her pocket knife and held it to Lisa's neck. You better believe Lisa kept her mouth shut after that. Jayna was a bad bitch. She did whatever she wanted whenever she wanted. She fingered a girl on a bus trip and beat up her ex-girlfriend because she cheated on her with a guy, to name a few things. Jayna was ruthless at times. Don't let her cute face fool you, she could be the sweetest girl, but she turned into a mega bitch when she didn't get her way- she was known to be a hot head. She even beat up a guy for Jenelle one time. Jenelle was talking to this guy name Lui. He was this cute Asian boy with the deepest dimples. He was nice to Jenelle, took her places, spent money on her and gave her head before she even gave him any play. One day Jenelle decided to give it up to Lui, but once he fucked her, he started to diss her. He told everybody she was a "loosey-goosey." Jenelle had been around so there could have been some truth to it but it isn't my pussy so it didn't affect me. He even went to the length of making a Facebook page boycotting her sex game and telling everybody her pussy smells. Jayna got so pissed, like if it was her pussy he was talking about. She waited for him in the bushes at his house one night and when he finally walked up to his door. She busted out of the bushes and jumped kicked him to the ground and took out her bat and started beating him with it. She said he cried like a bitch. She even spat in his face once she was done whipping his ass and ordered him to take the Facebook page down and walked away. The following morning the page was down and anytime Lui saw Jenelle he would put his head down and walk in another direction.

Jayna and Jenelle were not only known for their fighting ways, they were also known for their large sexual appetites, especially Jenelle. There have even been a few times when we would go to the club and she would find a guy to flirt with - ones who had money to buy her drinks and potential to become her sugar daddy. If she was feeling him, she would take him home and put it on him; I didn't like that shit, the risks she would take with these guys weren't safe. There are so many diseases and she didn't use protection all of the time. I don't know, maybe the fact that Jenelle and Jayna were both molested by their babysitter's son when they were eight had something to do with the way they were. They never really got proper help after it happened and started to rebel at a young age. Their mother was a single mother with two jobs, who left them with strangers sometimes because she had to go to work to provide for them. She became a stripper to start making fast money to make sure they had the flyest clothes, shoes and designer purses. She felt that buying them stuff would make them happy, but it only covered up their pain on the outside. Their mom was never there, they had no proper supervision and no father, which left them feeling empty; and if they continued to live this way, it was only going to get worse from here. People use to call them hoes due to Jenelle sleeping with other girls' men and Jayna taking a dude's chick and turning her out. They never let it faze them; they did whatever they pleased no matter what anyone said about them.

CHAPTER 10: WHAT GOES AROUND COMES BACK AROUND

School was a week away when Hazel called screaming and crying that she was in labor. The rest of the girls and I were at the mall going back-to-school shopping when we got the call, so we rushed to the hospital together. Leon was already there and was standing by the vending machines making a call when we arrived. We walked right past him and went straight to Hazel's room. Hazel was in pain and she looked horrible too. She was lying on the bed in the ugly hospital gown with sweat all over her face and no make-up on. The Doctor came in to check how far along she was, "You're about eight and a half centimeters dilated." Hazel yelled for the epidural, but the doctor advised her that she was too far along to receive it. As Hazel screamed in despair, the nurse advised us that we had to leave the room as it was overcrowded. We all left the room, with the exception of Hazel's mom of course, and I went to go and get myself something to snack on. Leon was still there and he was talking on the phone to some girl, I could tell by the tone of his voice and body language, not to mention I overheard him say, "I miss you too babe. I'll come see you later on tonight after Hazel has the baby." I was so shocked! We all knew Leon was a jerk but this was really low. Hazel was about to have his baby and he was about to go see another chick? But what I heard next was even more disrespectful. "Hazel is just the mother of my child- nothing more. You're my baby; you're the one I'm with all the time. I can't help that Hazel still loves me," Leon exclaimed. I desperately wish I never overheard Leon's phone conversation, but I know that even if I told Hazel, she wouldn't leave him. She would go looking for the girl and beat her ass until she left Leon alone.

Leon clearly had some type of spell on Hazel. As beautiful as she was, she could have had any man, at least one that would treat her right, but that never registered to her no matter how much people told her. As the saying goes, 'those that don't learn, shall feel', and Hazel was about to feel. When Leon ended his call, I hid in the corner as he walked back into the room. I got myself a snack and headed back to the waiting area to join the girls. I sat down in a daze after hearing Leon and his new girlfriend on the phone. Cora looked at me and asked what was wrong. I looked at her and as much as I didn't want to say anything, I told her what I just overhead Leon saying. Cora had a look of disgust on her face. Leena sat there looking surprised while Jayna and Jenelle looked at each other and smirked. "What did she really expect, seriously? Did she really think Leon was going to change because they were having a baby? She couldn't be that stupid," Jayna said. "Plus, she kind of deserves it if you ask me. She was fucking her best friend's man while she was with Leon," Jenelle added. As sad as it was to hear the girls speak about Hazel's situation, it was the truth. "I don't know what to do, should I tell her later?" I asked. "Personally, I feel that you shouldn't tell her, we didn't tell Donna when Hazel was fucking Pay," Cora said. We were all surprised to hear Cora being so blunt about her feelings, but she did have a point. "I hear you Cora, but our loyalty lies to Hazel, not Leon", Leena added. "Loyalty? What loyalty? To my knowledge, whatever loyalty we had to anybody in this crew is gone. When we hid such a horrible secret from one of our friends to protect another one of our friends, it made all of our characters questionable. I wonder, if I was Donna, would you guys have told me? I know Donna is the newest to our crew, but knowing me as long as you do, would you have told me?" Cora asked with concern. "Personally, if it was anyone of us, I would have mentioned it," Jayna said. Hazel's mother entered the waiting room, "He's beautiful!" Great timing, I thought to myself; our conversation was getting way too awkward. When we walked into the room, Hazel was holding her beautiful baby boy. "What's his name Hazel?" Leena asked. "Caleb," Hazel said with a smile on her face. We all took turns holding Caleb, gushing over his small hands, baby smell and cute smirk whenever we called him a cutie. As we all gathered gushing over Caleb, Leon interrupted and told Hazel a lie about him having to leave to help his friend get his car out a ditch. The whole crew gave him a rude stare because we knew he was telling a bold face lie. "Leon, our son was just born, can't someone else help him?" Hazel asked, sounding sad and desperate. There was no amount of begging that would get Leon to stay as he had a prior engagement. Leon gave Caleb a kiss and left without answering a teary-eyed Hazel. Not too long after Ms. Nelson also left, as she had work early the next morning and we told Hazel that we would follow suit so she could get some rest, but that we would return the following afternoon before she gets discharged from the hospital. Hazel sighed as this was her first time alone with the baby and she expected Leon to be there with her. The reality of her situation, or should I say life, had finally kicked in. As we walked outside into the hallway Leena asked, "So… Are we going to mention anything to Hazel, or is this the new way of being friends?" Cora interrupted, "I'm just starting to treat people the way they treat others. You guys can do as you please but I'm keeping this to myself, I don't need or want more drama in my life." I shrugged my shoulders saying, "I don't know… I need to think about it because no matter what I decide, I'm afraid there will be no escaping anymore drama my way and I don't need this shit again. I just don't want to be in the middle of it all over again. Things just started to get back to normal." "Well I have nothing to say because I'm not the one that heard it," Jayna said as she looked at me. I rolled my eyes and left to get a ride with Cora while the rest of the girls left with Leena.

On our way to my house, I noticed Cora had an uneasy tense look on her face. "What's wrong? And don't tell me nothing," I said to Cora. "I'm just stressed and have a lot going on," Cora muttered. "Like what, I'm all ears," I said. "Well Trey and I broke up... Ok, more like I broke up with him. The other night we were supposed to go out to dinner, and of course I got all dolled up only to get stood up. I probably waited on him for 3 hours before I decided to stop calling him and getting his voice mailbox. I fell asleep in my clothes waiting up for him to call me back with a damn good explanation," Cora explained. She continued, "I noticed a missed call from an unrecognizable number when I woke up the next morning, and when I called it back, I got the police station. I immediately hung up and started to cry. I knew Trey was in jail. That same night I had told him to come straight to my house, but he insisted that he had to help one of his boy's with something first. It's like I knew something was going to happen. Anyway his uncle posted his bail and now he's on house arrest until his trial." I'm so sorry girl. What did he get caught up in?" I asked. "Trey and his friend got caught with an ounce of weed and a key of coke," Cora sighed. As we pulled into my driveway, Cora broke down in tears. "Don't cry Cora. I know you're hurting, but you have to think positive and be strong for Trey," I advised her. "I know, but there's more." Cora took a deep breath and said, "I'm late. I didn't get my period this month." I was shocked because Cora never even told any of us about her giving it up to Trey. I didn't know what to say. I didn't even know Cora had lost her virginity, because Cora never told her business to anyone. She was always selective of who she shared certain information with. We were all friends; unfortunately, that didn't mean that everybody in our crew was trust-worthy. "You're the only one I told, I don't feel like I can trust anyone in the group," Cora confided in me. "I'm about a week late, but if I'm being honest, I'm not having this baby. Trey doesn't even know I'm pregnant, and I know if I tell him, he'll only pressure me to keep it. And, I feel like if I do decide to have this baby, I'll only disappoint my dad. Bonnie, I'm about to go to College and start my career. I have a lot going on and I just don't have time for a baby," Cora began to cry uncontrollably. I hugged her and told her that I would not tell anyone. Cora is my best friend and had always been a great friend to me, so I intended to keep my word, as no one should know her business unless she wanted to tell them herself. "I already made an appointment at the abortion clinic. I just want to get it over with," exclaimed Cora. "I understand Cora. If you want me there, I'll be there for you. I'm not trying to judge you and I never will. It's your choice and it's your body," I said hoping it might have made her feel a little bit more at ease. "Thank you Bonnie I needed that. I'm glad I told you because it was eating me inside." I hugged her again and told her to call me tomorrow so we could meet up so she didn't have to go through this tough time alone. I got out of her car and waited until she drove off to go inside. As I turned to go inside my house, I notice a car parked up the street with a girl sitting inside. It was a white Honda Accord, with black rims and dark tinted windows. My phone rang distracting me from everything. It was Drew. "Hey baby, what's up?" I whispered to Drew. "Nothing boo, what you up to?" Drew replied. "Just getting inside from the hospital. Hazel just gave birth to a beautiful baby boy named Caleb," I said smiling. "That's cool. Have you talked to Cora lately?" Drew asked. "Yeah… She told me about Trey. She's really sad about the whole thing. We were just sitting in her car talking about it. Have you talked to Trey?" "Yeah, I spoke to him. He's holding up. He has a really good lawyer, plus the lawyer is really close to the judge so he'll have a good chance of beating his charges," Drew said. "That's good to know, Cora will be happy to hear that," I responded. "How's Cora doing? Trey said Cora's been acting off. He said that she doesn't seem like herself," Drew brought to my attention. I paused for a quick moment and said, "Cora's cool, just nervous to start College I guess." "Bonnie, stop lying," Drew called me out instantly. "Babe, I'm not lying? We were even talking about it on our drive home just now. You can even ask her yourself," I said with confidence. "Alright baby, I believe you," Drew said with his deep voice. "Lovey, as much as I wanted to talk to you, I'm going to go to bed. It's been a long day and I have to get up early tomorrow," I said to Drew with my baby voice. "Ok, love you Bonnie." "I love you too." I gave him a kiss over the phone; he sent me one back and ended the call. I took off my clothes and slept in my bra and panties. I curled up in my bed and as I was drifting off to sleep my phone rang. "Hello..." I said sounding half asleep." I could here was breathing I hung up and put the phone on silent. After the day I had, I had to get my rest so I could be there for Cora the following day at the Abortion Clinic.

Cora came by my house bright and early looking like an absolute mess. She looked anything but ready to go through with the abortion, but all I could do was be there for her emotionally and to drive her home to rest after the procedure. Cora had dark spots under her eyes like if she hadn't slept for days. She had on a red 'just chillin' MC Apparel crew neck, black MC Apparel jogging pants, and white chucks. As soon as I got into her car Cora said "I know I look like shit," and put her vintage black Ray Bans on. "I understand. There is no need for an explanation," I muttered back. The right side of Cora's mouth turned up slightly and she pulled out of my driveway. On our way to the clinic Cora's phone kept ringing but she kept ignoring it. "Why are you avoiding Trey? Drew asked me about you last night because Trey had told him you've been acting weird," I mentioned to Cora. "I know, it's just...I can't be myself with him if I'm not real with him, you know. I know it's my body but it's only right that I tell him and let him have a say, but I can't help but be selfish this one time," Cora said with tears in her eyes. She continued, "From the beginning of our relationship all I asked from Trey is that we always honor three things; honesty, consistency and respect. If he knew what I was doing right now I would be breaking my own rules that I've implanted into this relationship. I feel like the biggest hypocrite," Cora expressed trying to hide the pain in her voice. "At least you realize your wrongs; a lot of people would just try to justify their wrongdoing and not think about the people they will be affecting. As your friend, I have to ask… Have you really thought everything through?" I asked boldly. "I've outweighed the pros and cons, and the pros outweigh the cons. I can't take on such a huge responsibility right now when I'm planning to graduate from high school and apply for University. I have a lot going on and I just can't disappoint my dad." Cora continued, "He sees Hazel and Donna with babies and feels sorry for their children who will be deprived of so much just because their parents didn't choose to accomplish high school and establish themselves first. I just don't want to lose our relationship and see that look of disappointment on his face." I put my hand on her shoulder as a sign of empathy. "I love Trey, he's my first love but I can't take the risk of being a struggling single parent… Children aren't cheap! With Trey's bad choice, I would have a good chance of raising this child alone. The uncertainty of this happening again doesn't sit well with me." Cora pulled into the parking lot of the clinic and parked her car into what seemed like the furthest spot away from the entrance. She slowly took the key out of the ignition and sat still in her seat, leaving her well-manicured hands on the steering wheel. "Cora," I called as I placed my hand on her arm. She looked at me with sadness in her pretty brown eyes. I comforted her with a hug. I could feel her heart beating fast and could only imagine the pain she was feeling. We got out of the car and walked into the clinic, holding onto my arm. Cora checked in with the receptionist who gave her some forms to fill out before the procedure. While Cora filled out the forms, I couldn't help but look around at the other people in the room that were all here for the same reason. One woman in her mid to late twenties was accompanied by a woman I assume to be her mother; and, a young Spanish girl and her boyfriend sitting across from us. The young girl was crying as she filled out her forms, as her boyfriend sat beside her lecturing her about all the reasons why she had to have the abortion. Cora handed in her forms and waited to be called. Forty-five minutes later they called Cora's name. She gave me her keys and wallet to hold and followed the receptionist into the back room. The vibration of my phone startled me. It was Drew calling me again, but I didn't answer in order to avoid the risk of him questioning me about my whereabouts. Cora walked out about 15 minutes later, signaled me to the exit with a nod of her head, and we got into her car without her uttering a word. "Where do you want to go?", I asked after adjusting the driver's seat and mirrors. "Anywhere, I don't care," Cora answered as she put her shades on and leaned her seat back. I started the car and drove to High Park to mellow out before driving Cora home.

The following afternoon I decided to go check on Hazel and the baby. I could hear Hazel and her mother arguing as I walked up to her porch and rang the doorbell. "Hey Bonnie," Hazel said while she opened the door to greet me inside. I said hello to Ms. Nelson and followed Hazel upstairs. Caleb was lying in the middle of Hazel's bed just chilling and wrapped up in his snug baby blue blanket. I love kids and I couldn't wait to have a few of my own someday. I sanitized my hands and went over to hold Caleb. "You ok Hazel? You looked stressed," I said. "Leon hasn't been answering my calls, Caleb wakes up every two hours in the night for his feedings, the house is a mess and my mom wants me to clean it even though I just had a baby. I have no energy," she replied as she gasped for air. "Don't worry, I'll help you," I said to Hazel. When Ms. Nelson left, we started cleaning the house from head to toe. I helped Hazel organize the entire nursery and packed away the baby's stuff from the baby shower, and then gave Caleb a bath and put him down for a nap. "Thank you so much Bonnie! I couldn't have done all of this without your help," Hazel exclaimed. "Not a problem Hazel, you know I got you." Hazel's phone rang and it was Leon. She answered, "Where have you been Leon? I've been calling you since last night." "I was out doing some stuff. Where's my son?" Leon asked as he ignored Hazel's question. "He's here sleeping," Hazel said sounding aggravated. "I want to take him to my house," Leon said. "Ok fine, I'll get ready and you can pick us up in about 1 hour," Hazel said. "No, not you, just Caleb," Leon replied. "What? Why? That won't work anyway because I'm breast feeding him so I need to be with him," Hazel said sounding pissed off. "You can use the breast pump you got from the baby shower," Leon suggested. As Hazel was about to respond, she heard a girl's voice in the background. "Who the fuck is that Leon?" Hazel yelled with anger in her voice. The girl grabbed the phone from Leon and responded, "It's his woman bitch!" "Who you calling a bitch, hoe! I'm the mother of his child; you're just a one-night stand!" Hazel clapped back. "One-night stand? Leon and I have been fucking for the past year and we recently decided to take our relationship to the next level. I guess you giving your pussy away to anyone with a dick made him come running to a real woman," the girl said arrogantly. Hazel was completely caught off guard; she was almost at a loss for words. It must have been serious if Leon's new girl knew about her and Pay's situation. "Fuck you bitch! Tell that low life that I'll see his ass in court you dumb bitches!" Hazel shouted and threw her phone across the room. "I can't believe he would do this to me. I just had our child. How could he treat me like this?" Hazel broke down sobbing uncontrollably. I walked over to give her a hug but she shrugged me off then immediately turned to accept my embrace after realizing what she had done. It was a bit awkward. I thought, why would she feel the need to push me away? I asked her if she would be alright because I had to leave to pick up my sisters from school and run some errands for my mom. Hazel nodded yes and thanked me again for my help and shoulder to cry on. I gave Caleb a kiss on the forehead and left. As I got in the car and drove off, I saw the same white Honda Accord that was at my house the other night. I drove by slowly and tried to get a look at the driver which appeared to be a woman, but it was hard to tell due to the tinted windows, so I just turned my head and continued driving.

On my way to pick up my sisters, I stopped at McDonald's to get them something to eat. When I went inside I saw Sean, one of the guys who chills with our crew. "Hey Bonnie, you look good. How have you been?" Sean said as he looked me up and down like I was a happy meal. "I'm fine Sean. I just came here to pick up some food for my sisters. I'm about to go pick them up from school," I answered. "That's cool. I hear you have a man now. I hope he's treating you right, I know I would." Sean said sounding like he knew he missed out on a good thing. Sean was in an on and off again relationship with his longtime girlfriend named Nikki. As much as I had a crush on him, I'm not the home wrecking type. I knew of her, and I've even seen her a few times. She was brown skinned and petite, nothing special if you asked me. She never dressed up or wore make-up. She just looked like she was going with the flow of life. "I know you have a man and all, but maybe we can chill one day and catch up," Sean said eagerly. "Yeah, one day," I said as I licked my lips. I'm a flirt, but a harmless one. I would never cheat on Drew, I know what I have and I plan on keeping it. I ordered my food and Sean helped me carry it to the car. I told him later, and he smiled as he watched me drive off to my sisters' school. I got there just as the bell rang. While waiting for my sisters to come out Drew called. "I've been calling you all day. Where have you been?" Drew asked sounding concern. "I'm sorry baby, I went to see Hazel and

67

help her out with the baby. She is really stressed out about Leon and keeping peace with her mom. I'm picking up my sisters from school right now. Plus, my phone's been on silent. I'm sorry." I said innocently. "If you're not busy later, I would like to come and kiss your adorable head and I'm not talking about the one on your shoulders," I said in my flirty voice letting him know he was about to get some. He snickered and said, "You know I'll always make time for you and those lips baby," Drew said sounding horny. My sisters jumped in the car so I told Drew we would continue our conversation later. "Hey girlies how was school today?" I asked. "Good!" they both replied in harmony. "I got you guys some Mickey D's, just be careful not to make a mess in Cora's car." My sisters were happy. When we got home, I told them they could watch a movie after they changed their school clothes. I started cleaning and making dinner for my family. I cooked jerk chicken, rice and peas and cauliflower. When I was done, I went upstairs to take a shower and get ready for my little date with my love. I curled my hair and put on my white see-through white MC Apparel Legit V-neck, a pair of black tights to show off my biggest asset, my leather rocker jacket and black strapped up heels. When my parents came home around 7 o'clock, I had dinner set on the table for each of them. I called my sisters to come down for dinner, hugged my parents and told them I was going to meet Drew and that I would be back around midnight.

When I pulled up at Drew's house he was outside shooting some ball. He was wearing his Jordan eighteens, ball shorts and no shirt. He knew I loved to see his muscular body. I walked over to him while he stood still and licked his lips and rubbed his face. I walked right up to him and he puckered up his lips for me to give him a kiss. I went on my tippy toes, wrapped my right hand around his head and made him lean in forward and kissed him slowly. "Hi," I said. "Hi," he said back. "You want to play a little one-on-one?", Drew asked

68

with a smile on his face. "Not in these heels, but we can play hide and go seek the pussy," I said laughing. He laughed too as he threw his head back and grabbed me close. He took my hand and led me inside his house. I said hello to his mom and chatted a bit with her and spent some time with his sister who was visiting from NYC. After spending time with his family, Drew interrupted and we went up to his room. I took off my jacket, sat on his bed and told Drew to come sit beside me. He said he wanted to take a shower first. "Come here. I like it when you're a little dirty,". He walked over and picked me up. I wrapped my legs around him and used my toes to push down his ball shorts. He laid me on his bed and let me feel his growth. As he pushed his self against me, I grinded back. Drew took off my tights and pushed my panties to the side. He forced his self in my tight pussy and the wetness helped him slip his dick in me with more ease, making my pussy becoming a mold of his dick. Using only his teeth, he pulled up my shirt and removed my bra with his left hand. I rolled him over and pulled my shirt completely off and took control. I saddled him and began to ride him to the rhythm of my own beat I was playing in my head. Drew moaned while grabbing my hips to push all of his self in me. Drew sat up as I continued to ride him and he sucked on my nipples, biting them softly, moving his way up to my neck then making his way up to my lips. He laid me down on my back and flipped me around to make love to me from the back, pulling my hair, biting my shoulders and pushing himself deeper into my pussy. I moaned so loud Drew had to cover my mouth. He then turned me on my stomach and continued to pleasure me. My hands planted on the bed, he put his fingers between mine and began to move faster and faster until we both came. He came off of me and turned me around to kiss me. We took a shower together and chilled for a bit before he walked me to the car. We made out some more before I left. "Call me when you get home baby," Drew said.

"I will lovey," giving him one more kiss before I left. I drove off and headed home with a smile on my face.

CHAPTER 11: FRIENDS OF A FEATHER FLOCK TOGETHER

School had started and I was ready for it to be over with. It was our last year in high school; Cora was starting George Brown College; and, Leena had decided to take a year off. I'm just hoping this year brings less drama, but I highly doubt it will play out that way. "Hey Bonnie!" Donna yelled out in the hallway. "What's up girl?" I replied sounding happy to see her, which I was. "What class do you have first?", Donna asked as she looked at her own schedule. "I have math with Ms. Bella," I love math so that was going to be an easy credit. "Cool, well I have English with Mr. Douglas." The first bell rang and I still didn't see Hazel. I sent Hazel a pin on her blackberry as Donna and I headed to our classes. She took a while before she finally read my message but she didn't reply. That was strange and quite rude I thought to myself. I put my phone away and paid attention to Ms. Bella. After class was over I went to my locker to get my books for my next class. Hazel came up behind me and tapped me on my left shoulder. "Boo! What's up?", Hazel said sounding happy. "Hey, just going to class. What's good? I sent you a message on BBM which you read but didn't respond to," I exclaimed. "I was busy getting the baby ready for daycare and my car wouldn't start,". Hazel didn't look like someone that had a horrible morning with the smile that was on her face. "Have you spoken to Leon?". "Yeah, were good. That girl just needed a better understanding on what position I play in Leon's life, and it's not just being his baby mother," Hazel said with confidence. As Hazel was explaining how that mess with Leon and the girl was straightened out, I could see the anger she had for her, it was written all over her face. It made me wonder what she would be willing to do to keep his new girl away. I have a feeling that it's only temporary, and I'm pretty sure Hazel felt the same way too. I told Hazel I would talk to her later and headed to my second period class. When the bell rang I went by the auditorium to wait for Donna. I had lunch, co-op and then a spare; this semester was going to be a breeze. I linked up with Donna and left school to pick up Nelly from the babysitter's. After picking up Nelly we went to grab a bite to eat. "I'm leaving Pay; I can't take his shit anymore. He doesn't help me at all. He's always out partying and I'm always hearing stories about him being with other girls. I basically take care of Nelly by myself; that is a clear indication that Pay is not needed in my life," Donna blurted out. It seemed like she really needed to get that off her chest. "At the end of the day, you have to do what's best for you and Nelly. If it's no longer worth it, then it's time to make the required changes, even if it's not what you wanted," I advised. "Where are you going to go?" I asked. Since her mom decided to pack up and leave town for a man that wasn't even claiming her, she had nowhere to go. "I've been on the waiting list for housing. I told them some sob story and called them every day until they finally found me a two bedroom apartment that I get to move into next week!", Donna mentioned with a sigh of relief. "Good for you Donna. I'm proud of you," I replied. We continued our girl talk and ate our lunch before she dropped me to co-op.

After school I waited for Hazel by the front entrance. While waiting, I received a text message from Sean: 'Long time no talk. You crossed my mind and I just wanted to see if you're ok.' As much as I was flattered, I didn't want whatever this was to get out of hand. Drew means too much to me to ruin a good thing. I sent him a text back that read: 'Hey friend. I'm good, just at school waiting for Hazel to finish class.' Sean sent another text back quickly: 'I can't remember what your face looks like. Can you refresh my memory?' I laughed because that shit was corny as hell. When we all use to chill,

Sean and I flirted with each other but never took it any further than that because he had a girl, and I let him know I don't get down like that. It's funny, all of a sudden I'm dating someone and he and his girl are off again and he's trying to get with me?! Mama didn't raise any fool. 'Have a nice day Sean. See you when I see you' I replied with a smiley face. I had no intention on seeing Sean anytime soon. As Sean and I wrapped up our conversation, Hazel finally showed up. "This semester is going to be hectic. All my classes are academic and I have Math, Science, History and Law all in the same semester…This is going to add even more stress to my life," Hazel vented. "You want a ride?", she asked. "Sure," I said as I followed Hazel to her car. Once we got in her phone started vibrating. She looked at it and pressed the end button. By the time she put the key in the ignition, her phone started to vibrate again. It must have been the same person because she looked at it and pressed end again. I raised my eyebrows as I put on me seat belt, not wanting to get caught up into any more of her drama. We drove to pick up Caleb first and then she dropped me to Square One mall. I took the GO bus to meet up with Cora at the Eaton Centre to do a little shopping and catch up on Cora's first day at George Brown College. "Hey Cora, I'm here!", I said through the phone, excited for some girl time. "I'm in Zara. Girl, you better hurry up, it's crazy in here! So many sales and so many fashionable items," Cora screamed with joy. I walked to over to Zara and spotted Gina standing in front of a store nearby. She clearly did some damage in the mall with all the bags she had in her hands. Then some preppy looking white boy walked over to her and gave her some serious tongue action. He was dressed from head to toe in Armani clothing and some spiffy looking dress shoes. He was tall, cute and looked like he comes from money, and that was probably what Gina liked most about him. She asked him to take her bags to the car so she could do a little bit more shopping. He gladly obliged taking her bags while slipping her his credit card to spend more of his daddy's money. I guess the white boy has expensive taste; meaning girls that sell their pussy discreetly, to be decked out in the finest of things. Sad and degrading, but this seems to be what today's society is all about. Gina then took out her phone and called someone. She sat on one of the benches in front of the store and I moved in closer to try to hear what she was saying. "What's going on?", Gina said to the person on the other end. Gina then asked, "So how is our little plan going? Do you think she knows anything?" This conversation sounded a little too familiar. "I'm with one of my sugar daddies," she said as she laughed. She carried on, "I know, but he isn't shit! I miss Drew. He's the one who has my heart and always will." The grace of God held me back from slapping that trick. If she really thinks that whatever conspiracy she has cooking to break up me and Drew, she had another thing coming to her, because that was never going to happen. I just had to figure out who she was using to try to mess up what Drew and I have. I knew that whoever it was would have to be someone close to me, but I just hoped that I'm wrong. I decided to leave before she saw me, but as I was leaving I heard her say to the person they would meet up tomorrow night. She hung up and I left as her sugar daddy returned. I met up with Cora and indulged in the sale at Zara. Cora and I picked up some dope pieces and then headed over to H&M. "Guess who I just saw?", I whispered to Cora. "Mickey Mouse?!", Cora said sarcastically. "No, but cute. I just saw Gina and her sugar daddy. I overheard her talking to someone about planning to break up Drew and me," I informed her. Cora's jaw dropped. "Is this bitch on drugs? Who plans on stealing someone's man? What a loser," Cora expressed. "That's not even the sad part. I've been feeling that she's working with someone close to me," I mentioned to Cora with great concern in my voice. "Well, we know it's not me," she said innocently. "You know you don't have to tell me that, I would never think it was you," I said with certainty. We finished shopping and headed to the parking lot to Cora's car. On the drive home I asked Cora, "So... How have you been feeling since the last time I saw you?" "I'm dealing with it. I try not to think about it to tell you the truth. What I did is making me push Trey away. He has been trying to communicate with me and I just can't face him," Cora said trying to hold back her tears while keeping her attention to the road. She continued, "I feel in order for me to move forward with Trey, I have to tell him the truth. Like I said, I wouldn't like him lying to me. I would prefer to hear the ugly truth than a beautiful lie". "I agree with that. You're not the type of person to tell a lie to the people you love. You're always honest, which is why this secret is eating at you." Cora looked at me and smiled. "That's why I love you Bonnie. You always understand me." As Cora and I continued our conversation, I felt my phone vibrating in my pocket. I pulled it out to see it was Hazel calling. "What's up?", I answered. She immediately asked, "What time are you going to be home?" I thought to myself, not even a hello? "Well its 7:30 p.m. right now, Cora and I are going to get something to eat, and then Drew and I are going out, so probably around 11:30 p.m." I wasn't going to dinner with Cora because we had already eaten, and Drew had his cousin's engagement party to go to. I was headed straight home, but I wanted to find out why she needed to know what time I would be home and what she planned on doing before I arrived. I let Cora in on Hazel's shadiness and told her I would call her later. As I was walking inside my house, I saw the same white Honda Accord roll up on my street. The driver parked the car but didn't get out. I stood at my front door, watching through the glass window. Then I saw another vehicle drive past the white Honda pretty fast. The person parked a couple blocks up. Whoever it was was dressed in all black. Something about this scene just didn't sit right with me. The person walked up to the passenger side of the white Honda and got in. They sat in the car and just waited. I started to think if that was the reason Hazel wanted to know when I was coming home. Was she trying to set me up? If so, why? I know Hazel did some fucked up things to her friends but she wouldn't go that far, would she?

They must have waited in the car for almost three hours. Hazel then called me, but I didn't answer, so she sent me a pin via BBM: 'Where you at? I wanted to have some girl time', it read. I knew she was lying, even via text message I could tell. I chose not to respond to that either. I guess they got tired of waiting, because 5 minutes later, the passenger got out of the Honda and went back to into their car. The driver of the Honda drove off first, throwing something out of the window. The other car then followed suit. I waited for a moment then went outside to see what the driver threw out their window. I walked over to find a cigarette bud with fusion pink lipstick. I know now that whoever it was, wasn't just a pussy, but also has a pussy between their legs.

CHAPTER 12: HE LOVES ME, HE LOVES ME NOT

School was going well, and I am determined to finish my last year with a 90% average or higher - I'm not fucking up my chances of getting into University at all. I intend on making something of my life. As much as I liked to party, have fun and be wild at times, I envision more for myself and I am bound to make something positively great happen. I was leaning towards a career in Psychology or as a Fashion Designer. I know, 2 completely different career paths, but I have an equal interest in both fields. Cora was loving College and making new friends in one of the courses she was taking; Jayna and Jenelle were also in their last year of high school; Leena was taking a year off before going to College; and, and Hazel was trying to fast track so she could get out of school and make things happen. Hazel would never do anything out of passion, it was more to prove something so people could think highly of her. She was showing more and more of how disingenuous she was. Plus, with her proving everybody right about having a baby for Leon, she felt that she had even more to prove; and apparently, she had decided to leave Leon. She said she needed something different, a man to treat her well; the same thing that we have all been telling her, but we were happy that she finally decided to get on the band-wagon. We all knew that it wouldn't be long before Hazel would be in another relationship; we called her a serial dater, because she had to be in relationship all the time.

To celebrate her new-found independence from Leon, Hazel wanted all her girls to go out and celebrate. Cora suggested we attend pub night at her school. Drinks, new faces and college boys, of course Hazel agreed immediately and the rest of us agreed. We all headed home to get ready and planned to meet up at Jayna and Jenelle's mom's condo and go to the pub from there. Cora showed up in a white mini skirt, a black turtle neck belly top and baby pink strappy shoes. Cora's hair was freshly dyed blonde, and she had smoky eyes and red lips. Hazel had on a red mini dress, leather grey heels and slivers studs in her ear. She slicked her hair back in a high bun, and wore false eyelashes with nude lips. Jayna wore black skinny jeans and a white blouse, while Jenelle wore black leather shorts with a see-through tank top and her hair in a short red bob. I wore royal blue skinny jeans with a see-through black shirt. I decided to be dangerous and not wear a bra and use black tape to put the sign of 'X' to cover both of my nipples. I wore my hair curly, and borrowed a pair of my mom's multi-coloured Prada shoes. Leena didn't feel like coming to the pub and it seemed like something was up with her… I guess time will tell.

We headed straight to the bar to get our drink on as soon as we got to Cora's college. We all took a few shots of Vodka while we waited for Cora, but Hazel was going in on her 6th shot before Cora came over with some of her new friends. "Hey girls! What's up? I want you to meet some dope people. This is Crystal, Desha, Anthony and Study", Cora said introducing her new friends us. We all said a friendly hello but Hazel had been a little too friendly with Study; he was Hispanic and African-American, 6'2 with a goatee, and looked like he was about something. He was pleasant and funny which made Hazel gravitate to him; but, of course there was a hurdle to overcome – Desha. Desha was Study's girlfriend. She was a simple but pretty girl with all natural hair which she wore in a ponytail, she didn't wear any make-up but she had great skin was a bit chubby, and judging by her wardrobe choice, you could tell that she was insecure. As Hazel flirted with Study, Desha became very annoyed and walked off. Study didn't look like the cheating type but then again looks are deceiving. Study thought Hazel's flirting was harmless, but he clearly didn't know Hazel. When she has her eyes set on someone or something, she goes to any length to make sure she gets what she wants, and Study was about to find that out. We danced the rest of the night with our drinks in our hand and had a few laughs as we got faded. I was definitely looking forward to College life, and couldn't believe it was less than a year away.

When we were leaving the Pub, Hazel couldn't be found; and to no surprise, neither could Study. Desha had this worried/angry look on her face. When we walked outside, Hazel and Study were sitting on the benches in the front laughing and talking. I guess Desha couldn't help herself and said, "Study, I'm ready to go." You could tell by her tone of voice that this guy done fucked up. Study stood up and told Hazel bye, but as he was leaving Hazel grabbed his phone and put her number into it. "Call me, friend," Hazel said in seductive manner. We caught a cab and of course on the ride home Hazel was gushing over Study. "He's so tall and sweet…", Hazel said sounding like a little school girl. "You know Desha is his girl, right," Cora said giving Hazel screw face. "I know, I'm not going to pursue him but he is very attractive, and I can't help who I'm attracted to," Hazel said slurring some of her words. We sat in silence for the rest of the way home feeling a nice high off the alcohol. I was really drunk and was horny as fuck, so I called up Drew but kept getting his voice mail. I sent him a text and waited for a response but I didn't get one. I had a strange feeling in the pit of my stomach that something was off. We got to the Twinzys condo and chilled for a bit. Hazel was on her phone texting someone while smiling and laughing. We all thought it was Study so we left her alone. Jayna rolled up a blunt and the rest of us went on the balcony to mellow out. We all hit the blunt and talked about how much we enjoyed ourselves and Hazel's groupie ways towards Study was discussed. Cora was pissed because she was friends with Desha and she is the one who introduced Hazel to her new friend's man. "How am I going to deal with this shit now?!", Cora asked sounding drunk out of her mind. "Why couldn't Hazel have set her eyes on a single man," she continued, this time laughing. I excused myself to go to the washroom, and left Cora, Jayna and Jenelle on the balcony laughing. I paused on my way to the washroom when I heard Hazel whispering to someone. "You did it?", Hazel whispered in her phone, trying to be as quiet as possible. She then laughed, "OMG! Wait til she finds out. It will be over for sure! Now we both get what we want." I continued walking to the washroom puzzled at what Hazel was up to now. While I was peeing a call was coming in from a private number. I answered it quickly thinking it was Drew, "Hello? Drew?" I waited for a response and heard nothing, so I hung up, washed my hands and went back on the balcony to chill with the rest of the girls. I kept looking at my phone the whole time, hoping for Drew to call. My desire for Drew's touch had faded. I played it cool as I continued to chat it up with the girls for another hour, until Cora decided she was ready to go. I got a ride with Cora and Hazel drove home by herself. During the car ride home I confessed to Cora, "I'm worried. I've been calling Drew and he hasn't called me back yet." "He's probably just sleeping," Cora responded. "Drew always answers my calls; it just doesn't seem normal. Something's not right," I said. My mind was racing trying to figure out what was going on with Drew. Cora pulled up in my driveway to let me out, and I told her to text me once she got home and she drove off. As I proceeded to walk to my front door, I saw a tall shadow start to approach me so I screamed. "Wait! Its only me." "Drew, is that you? What are you doing sitting on my porch in the dark? And where have you been? I've called, texted and you didn't return any of my messages?!", I began to ramble on. As I was talking I noticed an alarming look on Drew's face as if he had something to tell me. I stopped talking and looked at him. He looked away in shame. "Drew?", his name trembled out of my mouth. "I don't even know how it happened, I....", Drew was scared to go on. "Baby, I think I cheated...I was at a party, Gina was there, and I was drinking a lot and started to stagger so I remember that I went upstairs to lay down. Then it gets fuzzy, but the last thing I remember was Gina coming in and trying to kiss me. I pushed her off but I was really drunk and weak, and completely blacked out after that. When I woke up, I was in bed with no clothes on. Baby I'm sorry. I had to tell you, I fucked up but I didn't want to lie to you", Drew explained sounding remorseful and sincere. I could tell by the tone of his voice that he was desperate to get past this; but that didn't change the fact that I was hurt. I looked at him as the tears began to fill my eyes and walked towards my door saying, "I...I can't talk to you right now." Drew grabbed my arm. "Don't fucking touch me Drew! You said I had nothing to worry about with her. You lied to me. Please just leave me alone Drew...Please," I shouted. He let go of my arm and watched me walk inside. I walked upstairs and noticed that Drew was still standing in front of my door. I shut my room door and sled down behind it crying uncontrollably. I must have been sitting on the floor for about 40 minutes before I decided to try to pull it together and get ready for bed. I walked by my window and saw Drew sitting in his car. A small part of me wanted to run down to him and embrace him, but I was too hurt. I undressed down to my bra and panty and fell into bed.

Not even a full three hours later, my alarm clock went off. I was hung over, sad, depressed and feeling anti-social; I did not want to face anyone at school. I didn't want to explain anything to my friends; I just wanted to be left alone. My mom came in my room, "Bonnie, why aren't you getting ready for school?" "I'm not feeling well mom," I said as I put my head under the covers trying to hide my swollen eyes. "You sick or hung over? I heard what time you came in the house this morning. I thought I saw Drew's car. Did he stay over?", my mom asked. I rubbed my head and answered, "He was here but left." "What time did he leave?" my mom asked as if she was conducting an investigation. "Not too long ago, why?" I responded. "Because he's sleeping inside of his car in my driveway," my mom said and then closed my door like she knew there was something going on. A look of surprise came across my face when she said that. I jumped out of bed to look out my window. My mom was right. I couldn't believe Drew was sleeping in my driveway. I put on some sweats and headed outside. I knocked on the window hard startling Drew out of his sleep. He wiped the drool from the side of his mouth and opened the door. "Bonnie, I know your mad but I just can't leave here knowing that this is the end of us, please Bonnie. Tell me that we might be able to work this out?", Drew begged and pleaded. "Drew... I don't know right now. You hurt me. I don't know what to tell my family and my friends. I feel so betrayed. I still love you, obviously, but I don't know if that's enough to make me forgive you," I said with tears in my eyes. "Our love is strong enough babe, I know it is," Drew said sounding hopeful that he could persuade me to consider forgiving him and move on. "If our love was so strong, you would have kept your dick in your pants!", I yelled at him without thinking. I was so angry and just wanted to be alone. "Listen Drew, I need you to give me my space so I can think. This is a lot right now and I need to make the best decision for me, because clearly I'm the only one who will think about me and my feelings," I snapped back. Drew was taking everything in, but he knew he messed up and looked ashamed. "I know it doesn't mean anything right now, but I'm sorry of what I did to us baby girl, believe that. I'm going to spend forever making it up to you if you'll let me," Drew said looking me in my eyes. "I love you Bonnie." I turned away to hide the tear I could feel about to run down my face. Drew got back into his car and drove off. I cried a little more as I watched him drive away and

82

then went back inside. "You ok Bonnie?", my dad asked. "Ya daddy," I said as I ran upstairs to my room. I locked myself in my room all day with the blinds closed so it could be as dark as possible. I kept my phone on silent to avoid the world. As soon as I heard my family leave for the day, I grabbed my weed box and rolled up to calm my nerves.

A few days had gone by and I managed to shut out the world. I got up to reach for my phone and saw 48 missed calls, mostly from Drew, and a couple from my girls and a few from an unknown caller. Drew sent me many text messages apologizing for his actions and begging for me to speak with him. Maybe it was the weed or me needing space for a level head, but something about this whole situation with Drew just didn't sit right with me. I couldn't help but feel like there was more to the story. My doorbell rang and my mom yelled, "Bonnie, Cora is here." My mom sent Cora up to my room and warned her that something was wrong. Cora entered my room, "Damn! It's depressing in here. What's wrong with you girl? Don't you see my missed calls on your phone? I've been trying to get a hold of you these last couple of days, I'm worried." Cora sounded concerned. "I'm…" I tried to utter that I was OK but the lie couldn't come from my lips not to Cora at least. "things are just fucked up right now," I said sighing. "What's bothering you? You know you can tell me," Cora said. She was right, I knew I could trust her. I took a deep breath and started to tell her what went down with Drew. "Drew cheated?", Cora asked, not convinced even after hearing the whole story. "Sorry Bonnie, but I just don't believe it. I guess I'm in disbelief. I mean it's not in Drew's character to cheat", Cora said sounding baffled. "Plus, it doesn't make sense. Drew said he remembers pushing her off, blacking out and then waking up naked in the bed. Well whatever it is, the truth will come to light in due time. I know it will be hard, but try not to think about it too much," Cora said sounding positive. I rolled up another blunt for Cora and I to smoke. We spent the rest of the night laughing, making me appreciate Cora as a true friend.

CHAPTER 13: MENDING A BROKEN HEART

It had been weeks since Drew and I last spoke. He left me plenty of messages, called Cora numerous times asking if I had made up my mind, and even came by my house a few times hoping that I was finally ready to face him. I love Drew and I know he loves me, but if I go back to him without rebuilding the trust between us, it will only go downhill from there. I don't want to become one of those girls that call their boyfriend every five minutes because they lack trust in their relationship from one bad choice. That's not a healthy relationship. I needed to be able to trust, and maybe that would come in time. After thinking about Drew all day I decided to finally give him a call. Drew didn't answer, so I took it upon myself to go over to his house. "So this is why you can't answer your phone?", I said as I walked up to find Drew and Gina arguing in front of his house. Drew put his hands to his head as he knew it was only going to get worse from here. Gina had a smile on her face which heated something in me, so much that I jumped the bitch. I knocked her down to the ground with my fist, and went on top of her and started punching her repeatedly. She threw me off her and kicked me in my chest, and that's when Drew intervened, before I could put my foot in her face. He put me in the corner of his porch and yelled at Gina to leave. I gave her the evil eye and managed to spit on her as she walked by. She tried to get at me but Drew stood in between us. She gave up and started walking to her car. I watched her get into a white Honda Accord and drive off. Then it clicked to me, she was driving the same white Honda Accord I saw parked down the street from my house, and the same one I saw on Hazel's street. I stood there as it all started to make sense, but the thought of one of my best friend trying to sabotage my relationship was a hard pill to swallow. Drew grabbed me by the hand as I stood there in thought, "You alright baby?" "I'm alright," I said as I fixed my clothes. "Why was she here? To get another fix," I rolled my eyes sounding annoyed. "I know it looks bad but she came here unexpectedly. I wouldn't answer her calls so she just showed up. When she got here I told her to leave and she wouldn't. She was trying to tell me how much she missed me and wanted to be with me. I just couldn't get her to stop," Drew explained. I was even more infuriated. "Listen Drew, I came here to see how we could work this out but I'm not trying to deal with Gina and her bullshit. Coming here and doing this, it just makes me feel like it's not even worth it," I vented. "Baby please don't say that. I'm a mess without you. I feel like shit. I even look and smell like shit. I haven't slept or ate. It's like I can't function not knowing what's going to happen between us. I need you, I can't lose you Bonnie," Drew confessed. I wanted to grab him on hold him tight because I know he meant every word and I also yearned for his warm embrace. As much as Drew didn't want to lose me, I didn't want to lose him either. "I feel the same way Drew but you hurt me and broke my trust, and in order for us to get pass this, you have to make me feel like I can trust you again, I need to be sure that I can trust you. I don't want to be insecure thinking another girl can take my place…" "And you won't ever have to think that," Drew said interrupting me. I stood there looking at him knowing he was being genuine. "Alright…" I said walking over to him. "Alright?!", Drew said excitingly. "This doesn't mean that we're back together, but as of today, we will work on our relationship," I said to Drew. He smiled. "Can I hug you?", Drew asked moving in closer. We embraced each other. I missed him and I could tell by his hug, he missed me too. "You smell so good," Drew whispered into my ear. My heart melted by the sound of his voice. I wanted more than just a hug and I knew Drew was thinking the same way. He continued to hug me and then he began to make his way with his soft lips to my neck. As I began to become aroused, Drew began to rub his hands down my lower back moving his lips from my neck to my lips. The way Drew kissed me, slow and passionate, was making me want to show him how badly I wanted him too. "You want to come inside and chill?", Drew asked. We both knew what he was implying. "No. I think we should stop. You know once we get inside it's on," I said smirking. "Alright, I'll respect that. We're 'trying' to work on rebuilding our relationship and that's the most important thing," Drew said as he stood there with his dick at my attention. I licked my lips as I   looked down towards his manhood. "You see what you did to me?", Drew said laughing, I began to laugh too. "You're on pussy probation for a while until we figure things out," I chuckled. Drew looked sad but grateful that I decided to give us another chance. Drew pulled me in for a kiss. "Now in order for this to work, you need to remove Gina from your life for good. It's not you I don't trust, it's her. She wants you and probably won't stop until she breaks us up for good," I warned Drew. "That's not a problem at all. I don't want her around me anyway; and, if removing her will bring you back, I will do it without hesitation." Drew answered giving me a kiss on my forehead.

After I left Drew's place, I went over to Cora's house to tell her all about the drama between Gina and me and what Drew and I decided to do. Cora was happy to hear Drew and I were going to work it out. I asked Cora what was up with her and Trey. "Trey got off his charges," Cora said calmly. "That's good to hear, but what's going on with the both of you?", I asked. "He came to see me the other day and we had a long conversation about our future. We talked about him getting out of the drug game and making us work; and, we're talking about moving in together after my first year of college. It sounded all great but all I could think about while he held me from behind with his hands placed on my stomach was the abortion and how I betrayed his trust by not telling him. I can't be with Trey if I don't tell him the truth; so I did," Cora said. I looked at Cora waiting for her to tell me how he took the news. "I told him I had an abortion, and started crying immediately. He looked at me and sat in silence. I tried to explain all the reasons why I did what I did, and he could only look at me with sadness in his eyes." Cora continued, "I told him that my decision wasn't easy, and that I didn't want to disappoint my father and be a single mom taking care of a baby by myself while my child's father is behind bars. I didn't want to take our child to visit him behind a glass window." Cora informed me of the entire conversation that took place between her and Trey; and, how he was speechless and kept repeating: "Our baby Cora?" Cora cried as she told me that Trey was so distraught that he just got up and left. Cora added that as he was leaving Trey turned to her and said, "Did you ever think that I would have stopped hustling if I knew we were going to have our child?" Cora said that his words stuck with her and hurt so much that she started to regret her decision to have an abortion. Cora and I spent the rest of the day at her house, until the night crept up on us and she drove me home. I got home just in time for dinner. I chatted it up with my dad and mom and then played around with my sister. I had been wrapped up in all the drama, which I appreciated a nice night in with my family. When I was getting ready for bed, I realized that I had received a text message from Drew: 'I just wanted to check in and say goodnight Bonnie'. I sent him one back with a smiley face that read: 'Goodnight Drew'. I got in my bed and my phone went off again; this time it was a BBM message from Hazel: 'I need someone to talk to…I need to tell someone'.

CHAPTER 14: PRETTY LITTLE LIAR

After the drama the day before, I was glad when school came to an end. I noticed that neither Hazel nor Donna was at school this Monday, so I called Hazel to see what was up. She answered the phone in a low tone. I told her that I would be right over as I remembered her message from last night.

When I arrived at Hazel's house I listened to Hazel as I watched Caleb in his rocking chair. "I pinned you last night because things have gotten so bad. All the secrets and lies…I really fucked up." I looked at Hazel with a weird look as I waited for her to continue. "I went to pick up Caleb from Leon's house and he was there with his new girlfriend. His brother opened the door and yelled for Leon to come downstairs. Leon walked over with Caleb, while his girlfriend picked up his bag and blanket; and, I immediately turned into a psycho and told him to tell his girlfriend not to touch my baby's stuff. I started going off and told him that I don't want her around our son. As I was yelling she started to yell too, telling me to fuck off and stop being mad that Leon doesn't want me. I became infuriated and yelled out: 'Fuck you and Leon bitch! Thank God Caleb isn't yours!'", Hazel exclaimed. I turned my head and widened my eyes at Hazel, "Why would you say that? Do you want him to think that?", I asked. I waited for Hazel to reply but she just looked at me. "He is Leon's son… Right Hazel?" I asked again but Hazel just sat in her couch silent and tears began to roll down her eyes. "Remember Pay and I slept together around the same time I got pregnant. Prior to the fight with me and Leon I had been feeling sick but I didn't think much of it. When Leon raped me that night, the reason I let it happen was because I knew I was pregnant and I thought if I pretended the baby was Leon's, he would treat me better. I fucked up thinking that my plan would work," Hazel confessed. I looked over at Caleb and finally saw his resemblance to Pay. I looked at Hazel in shock and she looked away from me in shame. "Caleb is Pay's baby," Hazel said as she cried. Hazel continued to finish her story, "He stood there with Caleb in his car seat and looked at him. He said to me: 'I knew something was up you slut. You clearly can't keep your legs closed!'" "I can't believe I told him just because I was jealous of his stupid new girlfriend. What am I going to do Bonnie? Donna and I just started to repair our friendship, she would die if she knew Caleb was Pay's baby," Hazel said. "Honestly Hazel, I don't know what to tell you. Does Pay know Caleb is his?", I asked. "I think he does. When he came over a few nights ago, he was looking at Caleb weird as if he knew that he could be his," Hazel said. I shook my head and thought to myself how selfish and dangerous this girl was. As we were talking Leon started calling her, but she didn't answer. He must have called about twenty times while we were talking. I wouldn't be surprised if he was hiding outside her house right now. He filled her voice mail calling her all types of names and threatening to fuck her up when he saw her. Leon sounded more than angry, he sounded like a person out for blood. I got scared when it came time to leave and take the bus home, so I called Cora to ask her if she could come and get me. She said she would but because I heard that she was with Trey, I told her I would ask Drew instead. Cora and Trey needed time together to work things out. I called Drew and he was more than happy to come and get me. When I got off the phone with Drew, Hazel asked, "You and Drew are still together?" I looked at her puzzled that she would ask that because I didn't tell her anything. "Why wouldn't we be together?", I asked waiting for her answer. "I...only asked because I haven't heard you talk about him in a while," Hazel relied frantically searching for an answer. I knew that she was hiding something, but I let it slide because in due time whatever she was hiding would come to light, and she was already dealing with so much drama.

Drew finally arrived, so I hugged and kissed Hazel and Caleb goodbye and walked out to meet Drew in his car. He had a fresh line up and was dressed to impress. "Where are you off to?", I asked. "Nowhere", he replied with a smirk on his face. I noticed as he was driving that he was going in the opposite direction of my house, "Drew, you and I both know that my house is not in this direction." He looked at me and smiled, "I know, but I thought maybe we could go somewhere first." Drew was hoping I would play along. "I'm not dressed properly," I said. "Don't worry you look good," he said and continued to drive. We finally reached our destination and I realized we were at the new restaurant I wanted to try. Drew had his friend hook us up in the nicest section of the restaurant with a lavish menu already prepared for us. Candles were lit, while the song 'Stay' by Rihanna played in the background. Drew really went all out and I appreciated it. "So how was your day?", Drew asked. "It was good. I just went to school and then checked up on Hazel and the baby. How was your day?" "Oh it was ok. School, work and now I'm spending time with you," he said looking me in my eyes. I smiled flirtatiously. We ate and talked for hours, until we had to leave because Daniel, Drew's friend that hooked up the entire evening, wanted to close the restaurant. We thanked Daniel for the delicious food and headed to my house. As soon as I kissed Drew goodbye and went inside my house, I received a call from Hazel but I let it ring because I didn't want to come down from the high I was feeling from my romantic evening with Drew. My phone started to ring again, only this time it was a call from Drew asking if I wanted to sleepover at his house. "I'll agree on one condition. Don't try and pass second base because you won't hit a home run," I chuckled. Drew laughed and mentioned that he was waiting outside for me whenever I was ready. I grabbed my stuff, jumped in Drew's car and we drove to his house. When we pulled up to his driveway I noticed Gina's car parked a few blocks away from his house, Drew noticed as well and rolled his eyes when he saw Gina walking towards his car. "Are you really still here? He doesn't want you, so leave now before I have to beat your ass again," I yelled at Gina as I slammed Drew's car door and started to walk towards her. Drew pulled me back and told Gina to go home. "How could you just forget about what we had Drew?", Gina said desperately. "It's supposed to be you and me, not you and this bitch," Gina continued ranting. "You had your chance, now leave us alone," I said. Drew's mom came outside to see what all the commotion was about. "Gina? What are you doing here?", Drew's mom said sounding annoyed. "Just leave my son alone. He doesn't want you; don't you see how happy he is? I don't want to see you around here again; all you do is cause trouble," Drew's mom told off Gina. Gina was so embarrassed, that she apologized to Drew's mom and left. "Drew, I don't want this shit outside of my house again. The next time Gina comes back here, I will call the cops. There's a reason why I never liked that girl," Drew's mom exclaimed as she went back inside. Drew and I followed and headed straight to his room. "Do you see what I mean about this girl, she's crazy," Drew said. "I've had enough of her. I refuse to allow her to jeopardize our relationship any further. I got my baby back and I intend to keep it this way," he finished. I was happy to know he wanted Gina gone just as much as I did. "Don't worry love, I'm not going anywhere," I said to Drew. He was a good guy and I wasn't going to let Gina take him from me. "I'm happy you're here," Drew whispered. I'm happy I came lovey," I whispered back as we both held each other close and made love again and again.

As the sun began to rise on our face, we woke up in each other's arms and managed to have a quickie before hopping in the shower to get ready for school. We ate breakfast with his mom and then he dropped me off at school. "Later babe!", I said with a big smile on my face as I kissed him goodbye. As I was walking in, Hazel stopped me at the front entrance, "I've been calling you all night. So what, you couldn't answer because you were with Drew? Figures." 'Yes I was with my man, and I had a little dilemma of my own. You're not the only one with problems Hazel," I said giving her more sass then she gave me, which she didn't like at all. I changed the subject, "Anyways, what happened now?", I asked sounding completely uninterested. "I called Pay over after you left to tell him that Caleb is his son and not Leon's; and, he said he knew all along but was waiting for me to say something. He understood why I lied, and asked me if Leon knew. I told Pay that Leon knew that he wasn't Caleb's father but that I didn't tell him who Caleb's father was. I explained how it all came out and he shook his head and then asked me when I was going to tell Donna," Hazel paused. I asked, "And?" Hazel continued, "I couldn't give him an answer. I didn't want this whole feud with Donna and I to start all over again, so I told him that I didn't figure all of it out yet. He told me that I better clear the air with Donna before Leon finds out the truth and spreads the news like a will fire. Then Leon rang my doorbell and wouldn't go away. He looked so angry, and I was afraid of what he would do if he saw Pay, so I didn't answer the door and we took Caleb and headed to my room quietly." I couldn't help but wonder if Hazel slept with Pay again while Leon was waiting to beat her ass. "Leon was still outside my house an hour later waiting for me to appear, but was greeted by my mom instead, who I called and gave a head's up to about Leon being there. About twenty minutes later my mom got home to see Leon sitting on our porch. It took her about 3 seconds to threaten calling the cops before Leon took off," Hazel explained. I could hear the terror in her voice as she continued "I told Pay that it may be smart for him to sleepover with Leon on a rampage. I was scared that Leon was going to come back;

luckily, Pay parked in the plaza." When Hazel finished telling me what happened, I asked, "Did you sleep with Pay?" Hazel looked ready to lie to me, but she knew I would see right through that. "It just happened once since having Caleb," Hazel replied with a bold face half-truth. I knew she started sleeping with him again when she and Leon started having problems. "I don't want Pay, I have my eyes set on someone else," Hazel said. I had an idea who the unlucky conquest was - someone else's man. "You know he has a girl, right Hazel," I gladly reminded her, although I knew she didn't need reminding. "What are you talking about? If you're referring to Study your wrong," Hazel lied unconvincingly. She knew she wanted Study and was going after him whether he had a girl or not. Study had been with his girl Desha for 4 years, so I don't know what made her think that he would be a good catch. Hazel might be gorgeous, but her attitude and selfishness made her ugly. If she wasn't after Study, it would only be a matter of time before he found that out as well. "Speaking of Study, he sent me a text inviting me to a college party tonight that starts at 10 o'clock. Do you want to come?", Hazel asked. "I might reach later, I have a few plans with Drew first though," I responded. As soon as I mentioned Drew's name Hazel gave me a mean mug and I highly doubt she realized the facial expression she gave me. "Anyways, who are you going to the party with?", I asked out of curiosity. "Just Jenelle and Cora. Jayna isn't feeling good and no one has heard from Leena. I must have called her 10 times and she still hasn't returned my calls," Hazel answered. "I've been meaning to get in touch with Leena. She's been missing out on all the fun for a minute now," I said to Hazel as I looked down at my phone to check the time. I told Hazel I would see her later and headed to class.

After school, I headed to Leena's house because it was unlike her to avoid our calls for so long. I rang the doorbell and her mom answered. "Hi Mrs. White, is Leena home?" I asked. Without answering, she invited me in and we sat down in the living room and explained Leena's absence. Leena was in rehab. I knew it was going to happen, with her being with Ray and his cocaine sniffing, pill popping ways. "Leena has been hiding it from you guys for a while, that's why she's been so distant," Mrs. White explained trying to hide the sadness in her voice. As sad as I was, I wasn't surprised, because Leena was a complete idiot when it came to Ray and all he ever did was bring her down. I was in tears leaving Leena's house. I felt like the worst friend in the world. I must have cried all the way home. I called Hazel, but got no answer, and my phone died as soon as I walked inside my house. I ran upstairs to tell my mom what happened to Leena- I needed someone to talk and my mom was a good listener. We talked for hours and I told my mom that Mrs. White mentioned that Leena was allowed visitors on Wednesdays and Fridays from 3:00 p.m. – 4:00 p.m. My mom said that she would come with me for support. I excused myself and went to call Cora and the rest of the girls, but I didn't get a hold of any of them. I'm guessing that they were all at the party. I decided to stay home as I was in no mood to have a good time knowing my friend who loves a good party was battling a drug addiction. I sent Drew a text and told him I had to take a rain check and he understood. I went straight to bed and waited to tell the girls what was going on with Leena.

The following morning, I noticed I had a few missed calls; 1 from Drew, 2 from Hazel and 1 from Mrs. White. I called Mrs. White first, "Hello Mrs. White. How are you?" "I'm good. I was just calling to tell you that I told Leena that you would visit her next week. She was upset at first, but then lightened up. What day should I schedule your visit for?", Mrs. White asked. "Please put me down for Wednesday at 3:00 p.m. Thank you Mrs. White." She thanked me for being a good friend, but I surely didn't feel like one. We came off the phone and then I called Cora to let her know what was going on with Leena. "Hey Cora, I was calling everybody yesterday but no one answered. Leena is in rehab." Cora was shocked and asked if I was joking. "Nope, Ray got her on that coke," I said becoming overwhelmed with emotions all over again. "You've got to be kidding me. Leena is doing cocaine? Since when?", Cora asked. "Her mom said she's been on that stuff for the past couple of months," I replied and continued explaining. "We all haven't seen Leena for a while. She kept blowing us off and we never really questioned it until the other day. I'm going to see her next Wednesday at 3:00 p.m. with my mom. Let me know if you want to come so I can tell Mrs. White." Cora was more than willing to join me to show our support to Leena. She then started filling me in on the drama that happened the night before. "Girl, there is something truly wrong with our friend," Cora began. I already knew she was talking about Hazel. She continued, "We got to the party around 11:30 p.m.; and, drinks were flowing and the vibe was right. We saw Crystal there dancing with some guy and Jenelle decided to go find herself a College boy to flirt with, while Hazel and I went over to chill with Study. The look in Hazel's eyes when she saw him was ridiculous- you could tell she wanted to jump his bones badly. We said hi and I asked Study where Desha was and he said that she had an exam to study for so she wouldn't be joining us tonight. Hazel had a grin on her face, and I didn't stick around much with the both of them gushing over each other, Trey ended up coming so I hung out with him for most of the night. Hazel and Study went to dance when her song came on and she was grinding all over him and Study looked like he forgot he had a girl. He was into Hazel and it looked like he wanted to take it a little further. After they danced to a few more songs Hazel and Study went for a walk away from the crowd. They were gone for a while before they came back to join us. Hazel's hair was messy and her shirt was not properly buttoned up, and Study's fly was down. We all knew she fucked Study; she clearly didn't give a fuck and it showed.

CHAPTER 15: BACK-STABBER

After Cora told me about Hazel's man stealing ways, I had absolutely no interest in talking to her. It was just embarrassing. Cora had just introduced Hazel to Study and Desha, and Hazel immediately started pushing up on yet another girl's man and was sleeping with him like it was nothing. I felt sorry for Cora because she had to face Desha knowing that one of her best friend's screwed her man, yet again keeping another damaging secret from a friend. Hazel was making our crew look bad; and, I don't know if she realized or even cared how all of her lies were badly affecting everyone who had knowledge of her deceitful ways and others who would just simply be hurt by her actions. Moreover, the fact that we had to cover for her also made us into liars and made us feel terrible - like history was repeating itself, but this time instead of Pay, it was Study. Hazel clearly didn't care about the back stabbing she was doing. She felt that nobody would hold her accountable for breaking up yet another relationship and that we would simply turn the other cheek as we've done in the past. We were all starting to see Hazel's true colors and even started to question our friendship with her since she didn't seem to have a loyal bone in her body nor morals.

After I spoke to Cora I called Hazel to let her know about Leena. "Hello?" Hazel answered her phone as she sounded like she was just getting up. "It's Bonnie, Leena is in Rehab," I said. I heard a male voice in the back and some giggling. "Hello, Hazel did you hear me?" I asked. "Oh yeah, sorry I was talking to someone. Why is Leena in Rehab?" she asked, even though she sounded more interested in the person she was with. "Ray got her hooked on cocaine," I said. "Oh really? How is she?" Hazel asked as she laughed with whoever was in the background. "Who are you with? I'm trying to tell you something important and you don't sound concerned. Leena is one of our best friends," I raised my voice, irritated at the lack of compassion Hazel was expressing. "I am concerned; it's just that I already knew Leena was on that stuff. I was there when Ray made her try it," Hazel exclaimed like it was nothing. "What? And you didn't tell any of us? We could have helped stop it from getting out of hand. Why didn't you stop her when you saw her doing it?" I asked, puzzled by Hazel's behavior. "Leena's a grown ass woman. Ray asked me if I wanted some and I said no, Leena could have said no too," Hazel said with no emotion. I couldn't believe what I was hearing come out of Hazel's mouth. Everybody in the crew knew Leena was weak for Ray. As strong minded as she was, she was human and had weaknesses too. I told Hazel we were going to see Leena on Wednesday and let her know if she wanted to come she could with all of us. After that I immediately hung up the phone. I was so pissed off at Hazel for being so uncompassionate. How could she keep something like this from us all and not try to seek help for our friend? On top of this, she chose to fool around with Study while her friend is in rehab, in part of something that she could have prevented. Calling Hazel a back-stabber would be an understatement.

CHAPTER 16: BLACK ROSES

The week flew by and it was time to visit Leena. I didn't want to see her in such a fragile state and I know she didn't want to be seen as a drug user. I know we smoked weed, but in my eyes, that was harmless. Cora, Jayna, Jenelle, my mother and I went to go see Leena that afternoon. When we arrived at the Rehabilitation Centre, to our surprise, Hazel was already there waiting for us at reception. By the way she was acting the previous day, I didn't even think she cared enough to show her support by coming; and, although she did show her face, that's all it was - there was nothing genuine about her being there. The receptionist paged Leena to let her know that her scheduled visitors had arrived and then directed us to the waiting area. When Leena came out to greet us, she looked skinnier than ever. The last time I saw her she had meat on her bones; I guess that coke got to her quickly. "Hey guys" Leena said with a half-smile. I know she didn't want people seeing her like this, that's why she stayed away for so long. I asked her how she was doing and she replied, "I'm ok...I guess." Leena sounded really depressed. "You don't sound ok," said Jayna. "Why didn't you tell us Leena? We would have done everything to help you?", Jenelle asked as she was very concerned. We all know cocaine is one hell of a drug, Leena clearly missed the memo. I don't know how Leena could have let Ray manipulate her into doing it. I know she was crazy in love with him but for her to give into it after seeing its harsh truth first hand is a mystery. Leena started to ramble on about how sorry she was for hurting herself and her family. "When I get out of here, I'm going to get my life back on track. Fuck Ray!" Leena had so much anger in her voice. Leena continued, "He didn't even come to visit me in here and it's his fault...

More like my fault for allowing him in my life for so long. I kept trying to save him when I should have been saving myself." Leena began to poor her heart out to us, and we all tried to be as supportive as possible by listening to her vent. Hazel, on the other hand, was all up in her phone texting Study after their little affair. Hazel pretended to be paying attention to Leena when all she really cared about was when she was going to see Study again. We spent the next couple of hours with Leena until visiting hours were over. After being in Rehab for about 5 weeks, she was being released on her own recognizance on Friday. We were happy that she was thinking straight, I just hope that this time she will stick to her word once she gets out. That's when the real test will begin; staying away from drugs, Ray and anything else that will lead to her self-destruction. We were all hoping that Leena would stay on a steady and clean path and not go back down that road.

The next few days were busy; I was focusing my attention on school, Cora was studying for her mid-term exams, Jayna and Jenelle were trying to take school seriously, and Hazel was on a manhunt for someone else's man. As Sunday approached, Jayna, Cora and I made plans to go visit Leena at home. Since she left rehab on Friday, we didn't hear any word from her. Cora picked me and Jayna up and we headed to Leena's. When we pulled up to Leena's house there were about five cars in her driveway and I noticed three police cars parked beside the curb by her house as well. When we got out of the car, we saw Mrs. White crying hysterically. Leena's aunt Rachel came over to us and said that Leena came home Friday but then left some time after with Ray. Before Rachel could finish explaining, the ambulance drove up and the Paramedics rushed in Leena's house with a stretcher, we knew it was bad. We ran over but the cops held us back. A few moments later, still with unanswered questions, the Paramedics came out with a body on the stretcher. We all began to scream and cry, we knew it was Leena. She was pronounced dead upon arrival.

We rushed back over to Rachel screaming for answers. "Leena came home Friday morning and by late afternoon she was gone. She came back last night out of her mind," Rachel explained trying to hold her tears back. "Leena and her mother got into a fight, presumably about Ray, and she stormed out. Leena came back with Ray and her mother called the cops on him and they arrested him on Saturday night. Leena was beyond mad with her mother and was freaking out that Ray was in jail." Rachel chocked back more tears and continued. "Her mother said she went upstairs and locked herself in the washroom and would not come out, even after she kept banging on the door and demanded for Leena to come out. They argued until my sister realized that Leena had stopped yelling back. She broke the door down only to find Leena laying on the floor with lines of coke on the counter." Rachel further explained that Leena's mom called the police as she tried to revive her, and then called her dad who immediately rushed home from work. She had overdosed on cocaine. Cora, Jayna and I sat on the curb in disbelief. Our friend was gone? We had just seen her a week ago and she sounded like she was ready to get her life back on track and move on from Ray, but she ran right back to him as soon as she came out. The fact that we lost a friend tonight wasn't registering with me. I didn't want to believe it but I had no choice but to accept it. We stayed with Leena's family for a while grieving the loss of our dear friend. I felt it for Mrs. White as no parent should have to bury their child.

CHAPTER 17: DARK SECRETS AND DEEP LIES

It's been months since Leena funeral and it's still hard to grasp. The crew and I checked in on Leena's family every now and then. The girls and I became even closer; the thought of us losing another person scared us, some more than others. Hazel was sometime-ish. One minute she was devastated by the situation and the next, it's like she didn't care. She became even more involved with herself and her own situation. Her and Study are still fucking, plus she messes with Pay when Study is with his girl and she still runs down Leon even though he still treats her like shit. Her and Leon where a never ending story, Leon was still with his girl but Hazel thinks she has some type of power because she Leon's baby mother. She clearly misses the memo that a kid cannot keep a man around. Now a days, some girls turn there pussy into a hustle, to get whatever they want from whoever they have their eyes set on. Hazel seems to be turning into one of those girls and in due time she will see the dead end it will lead her too. Hazel's little love triangle was about to get her into some hot water. Other than Hazel and her bullshit, Cora finally got back with Trey and their working on their relationship, she's working hard in school, Jenelle finally got herself a man and stop messing around with these lame boys, Jayna even got herself a girlfriend. Her name was Crystal, a mutual friend of Cora and Study's. They meant a couple month when Jayna and Jenelle went shopping. Crystal was a sexy girl, the way she carried herself, walked, talked and dresses, she was serious eye candy I even had to slap Drew upside the head a couple of times for staring to hard but I understood why. Shit, I even caught myself looking at her a few times. But the day Jayna seen Crystal, she just couldn't resist. She approached her with confidence and persistent, determined to get to know her better. Crystal has dark chocolate skin like Kelly Rowland, pretty eyes and a cute smile and an amazing body. She has a very pleasant outgoing personality, very likeable and cool to chill around. Jayna must have been draw to that because she got pretty serious with Crystal quick cutting off her pimp ways at the drop of a booty. Jayna seem head over for Crystal and wasn't afraid to show it which was different from how she usually handled her lady of choice. When Jayna first tried to talk to Crystal, she played hard to get and Jayna wasn't use to that, Crystal made her work for it and she respected that which she wasn't accustom to that. Just a few months into dating Jayna had Crystal meet her mom and she even brought her around to chill from time to time. We all liked her, well not all of us. Hazel doesn't seem too interested in getting to know her. I personally believe because she a stunning girl and Hazel felt threatened and since her and Study were sleeping around she didn't want Crystal to go and tell Study's girlfriend, Desha. I even notice when Jayna would bring Crystal around to chill, Hazel all of a sudden had something to do and places to go. One time we all were going to the movies and she had agreed to come prior too but when she found out Crystal was going, she bailed coming up with some story about the baby. I know it wasn't only for that. Hazel always us to tell us how her and Study would make it official soon, I don't know who she was trying to prove that to, us or herself? His phone was even in Desha name plus Desha and Study had promise rings which Study only wore when Desha was around and when he didn't wear it, it was him and Hazel had their sex session. We all know he did not plan on leaving Desha, everybody knew that but Hazel. I feel she knew she just didn't want to acknowledge it. At times it was a thrill for her she even said to me one time "I don't know what it is, but I like when other girls' men like me." All I could do was shake my head. She was one of my best friends but I was starting to question, why? The shadier she became the more I felt I couldn't trust her and wanted to even distance. Hazel even got so caught up in her love triangle; she neglected her motherly duties sometimes, making her mother pick up the slack when it came to taking care of Caleb. The person she was becoming was not likable, or is this just the person she always was?

Summer was approaching and we were about to graduate. That day couldn't come any sooner. I was so over high school and all its drama. I was getting ready to register for University but I was still unsure of what I want program I wanted to take. I didn't want to be that student that became so undeceives that I end up taking all the programs the school has to offer, I wanted to be sure it was going to be beneficial start to my future. Plus my parents already warn me about wasting their hard earn money. My parents work very hard for my sisters and I to have a good life and I appreciated that and I wanted to make them proud. We've almost been dating for a year and things are still good. We have are petty agreements but we never went to bed mad at each other. Drew wanted me to apply to the same school which crossed my mind a few times but I didn't want to be up his ass and I didn't want him up mine. I love him but I value my alone time, it's good for you and it keeps the relationship fresh but I did tell him I would think about it. Speaking of school Jenelle had decided to drop out since she got a full time job plus she had no chance of graduate. Her mother didn't object to it as making money was something she taught them from young. Their mother didn't even give them much supervision, allowing them to make their own decisions without needing her consent. Making money was the only thing she cared about. Cora and I tried to talk some sense into her but friends could only do so much. We tried hard to talk her out of it but it went in one ear and out the other. Although education is key, Jenelle on the other hand felt that money is the key to everything then again you are a product of your environment. Now Jayna on the other hand was making a few changes to her life. After getting with Crystal she started to become more focus, I gave Crystal credit for this as she seemed to be rubbing off on her. Jayna started attending her classes, getting her assignments done, even going home at a descent hour. Crystal had that pussy power; Jayna would tell us that Crystal would withhold her kitty cat until Jayna did her homework or to make sure she studied for exams. According to Jayna , Crystal was a freak, she would use whips, hand cuffs, blind folds even toys and I'm not taking about the ones kids play with. One time we went out for dinner and drinks, Jayna and Crystal decided to leave early, Jayna told us that they played a game while driving home. Every time Jayna got to a red light she would lick her pussy until the light turned green. Apparently Crystal had a golden tongue. The way she ate pussy had Jayna Cuming instantly. Jayna had mention that no girl made her toes curl as she was always the dominate one in any relationship but Crystal took that position and Jayna. Crystal got Jayna on a good page; she was focus, for once unlike Jenelle with her dropping and out and still partying hard until she finally met someone to tame her wild ways. His name was Jermaine, he wasn't very attractive but he had money and I'm not talking about a few thousand but millions which was a golden ticket for Jenelle and her lifestyle. He's completely opposite to her and he's older too. He's a recent grad from York University; he majored in accounting and comes from a long line of accountant money. I hear his family owns a large accounting firm in Toronto, New York and LA and he planned on joining the family business. Jenelle always said she would be with a rich man and now her dreams were coming true besides from that she seemed to be interest in him and he adored her. They have only been dating for a month but seem to be enjoying each other's company. But the only problem Jenelle had with him was his small penis and his sex game was weak. He was a missionary type of guy. He pulled no tricks in the bedroom but that didn't stop Jenelle from pulling out hers especially her secret weapon, her dick sucking game. Jenelle built a bad rep off a sleeping with other girls' men. The amount of fights we had to back her up in cause some girl decided to confront her about sleeping with her man was ridiculous ad but she had an even worst time keeping the bug-a-boo's away after she laid it down on them. She had skills when it came to sucking dick and she loved to flaunt it. Jenelle would go for hours and make a guy cum a hundred times and Jermaine was no exception. Although he sucked at knowing how to satisfy her needs. You can always tell when Jenelle put her head game on Jermaine cause she would always have something new. A new bag, shoes, jewelry whatever, he had Jenelle decked out, I even borrowed some of her clothes sometimes, some of the stuff still had tags on it. Her mom loved Jermaine for obvious reasons, showering Jenelle with lavish gifts and her mother sometimes. Her mother went as far as asking if he had a single relative. He spoiled her rotten and she loved it. Everything seems to be alright with everyone besides us losing Leena a few months back we had to find still live our lives. Some of us hand a harder time dealing with it Cora isolated herself for a little while she even distanced herself from Hazel a bit too. She felt she was responsible and so did I. Hazel must have been thinking so to because she became depressed after reality hit hurt, not that her friend just died but that she was somewhat responsible. There seem to be more to the story that Hazel wasn't telling us. After Leena's funeral, Hazel never grieved with us she grieved alone. One thing that I noticed is after Leena died we all hated Ray more than we had before but Hazel still kept in contact with him, I've seen his number multiple times calling her phone. There other morning she came to my house for us to get our nails done, we were upstairs in my room and she had went downstairs to warm Caleb a bottle before we left. I heard a text message alert from her phone, I being nosey took the phone out her bag to give to her and looked at the screen and notice Ray had texted her. "Hey beautiful" I was floored. Why they heck would Ray be texting Hazel that? Hazel should be just as angry with Ray as we all were. He's the one that got Leena on Cocaine which lead to her overdoes. I ran downstairs half dressed "Why the fuck is Ray texting you" I said boldly. I was so angry I don't even care how I said it I need answers and I wanted it know but when I asked Hazel she dropped the Caleb's bottle of milk and grabbed her phone out of my hand. "Why are you going through my stuff" she said sounded worried. "Hazel, answer the fucking question, I'm not letting this one side! Now tell me why is Ray texting you? He's the reason one of our best friends is dead" I said aggressively demanding an answer immediately. She looked sad and sat down. "That night Leena and I went to a house Party with Ray and some of his friends, we drank, smoked, we were just having fun like we usually do but we ended up taking things to a whole another level." Hazel said; as she continued her story "Ray took out a ball of coke and broke it up into lines in the bedroom table. He didn't even care who was looking, Leena complained but she was too drunk to enforce him to stop. That night, we were all really wasted. Leena wasn't the only one that tired coke for the first time that night, I did to" I was shocked to hear Hazel say that. Not only did she watch Leena do her first line that eventually lead to her death but she join into. Hazel continued "After we did our first line, we were on cloud 9. It was a different kind of high, a high that we all enjoyed. We did plenty of lines that night, the higher we got the more wild the party became" as Hazel was telling the story, I began to become not only pissed with Ray but with Hazel. Hazel then continued to fill me in "We were in the master bedroom and the music was playing and everyone was having a good time. Leena and Ray began to make-out, I don't know if it was the drugs or the alcohol but

I started to watch Ray seen me looking and whispered into Leena's ear. Leena looked at me and told me to come over to her and Ray on the bed. I went; Ray began feeling on my breast, while Leena began to feel on my thighs. I've never done anything like that but I was enjoying myself. It went from kissing and touching to me and Leena doing stuff. Ray video tape and said we were going to famous. As he watched he continued to video tape Leena and I fooling around. He then joined in and we…we had a threesome" by the time Hazel finished telling me the story I was stick to my stomach as I did not expect to hear all of that. That was a deep dark secret that all three of them were hiding. "Bonnie, Ray is threating me. She said He will expose the tape and everyone will blame me for Leena's overdoes. In the video it wasn't just us having sex but its shows me doing lines of coke off Leena stomach. I didn't know what I was doing at the time until Ray showed us the video, but it's done and I can't take it back." Hazel said as she started to cry. I didn't even feel sorry for her, I only felt disappointment. I found the courage to ask "So what are you doing in return to stop the tape some circulating" I waited for a more shocking answer. She was silent for a good a minute before she said "I've been having sex with him." We've only done it a few times. I'm always trying to find a way out of it but he always finds a way to make sure he gets what he wants" I was so in shock that I cancelled our nail date. I couldn't hide the disappointment I had for Hazel and she noticed. "Bonnie, what do I do?" I stood there and just shuck my head "I don't know. You made your bed and now you have to lie in it." I went upstairs and shut my door. Hazel took Caleb and left looking sad but I didn't care. You hide such a nasty secret that lead to our friend's death. There's no coming back from that. I looked out the window to see Hazel getting in her car. Once she got in, she texted me; "I know your upset with me and have all reasons to be but please, please don't tell the girls. I just need some time to find a way to tell them" I read the text and didn't reply. She stayed in the driveway and waited for me to confirm I was keeping her secret I was so mad, I couldn't even reply if I wanted too, she noticed that I wasn't agreeing to her dirty little secret and left. Now Hazel's love triangle had turned into a love square.

CHAPTER 18: FRENEMIES

After Hazel's confession I ignored her cries for help. I know she was ashamed of herself but forgiving her was the last thing on my mind. I was ashamed to call her my friend. She took it too far this time and I didn't want to be a part of it. I didn't tell any of the girls even though Cora questioned why I would always have something to do when I knew Hazel was going to be present; of course I just brushed it off saying that I was really busy and focused on finishing my last year of school strong. I decided that this was a secret I was keeping to myself. It was too dark of a secret for me to be the one to tell; plus, it was time for Hazel to start taking responsibility for her own messes.

Jayna and Jenelle's birthday was approaching and they were turning the big eighteen! Everyone was going to be there which will unfortunately include Hazel. The week before the Twinzy's party, Cora and I planned a double date with our guys, so of course this meant we had to go shopping. Trey and Cora have been working on their relationship after she told him about the abortion and things are going well between them. Cora has mentioned that their bond is tighter and he understands why she had the abortion. I'm glad they got back together because they balance each other out. I know Trey has a few big changes to make, but with some good loving and influence from a good woman, Cora would set him on the right path. After spending some serious bread in Zara, we agreed to meet around 8:30 p.m. for our double date. I put on my new outfit - a white and black romper pants suit with spaghetti straps and a cute white jacket to throw over if it got too cold. I wore my hair in a fish tail braid, light make-up with Mac lip gloss and my new stiletto heels. By the time I was ready, Drew arrived. I told my family that I was leaving and locked the door. Drew was waiting at the passenger side door, and opened my door for me like a gentleman. Before I got in I planted one on Drew. He held me by my waist and pulled me in again. We met up with Trey and Cora at Steph's House, a Jamaican restaurant that served the best West Indian food in the city. Drew and I interrupted Cora and Trey's lip-locking session before we headed inside the restaurant and waited for a waiter to place our order. "Hi! I'm Michelle and I'm going to be your waiter today. What can I get you to drink?" I ordered lemon water with oxtail and rice and peas, while Drew, Cora and Trey ordered a round of Coke and bbq jerk chicken and rice. I went to the washroom to wash up before our dinner arrived and heard a voice on my way say, "Hey you!" I turned around and it was Sean in his chef uniform. "Hi," I said startled. "You're chefing it up here?" Sean nodded "Impressive. How's everything with you and your girl?" I asked. Sean laughed, "I don't have a girl. I'm single," Sean said as he looked me up and down, licking his lips. "You look good by the way. Are you still with your man?" Sean asked with a grin. "Yes I am, and speaking of my man he's here with me now. We're on a double date with Cora and her boo," I said shutting his hopes down fast. "It's nice to hear that you guys are still going strong," Sean said with no real effort in trying to sound sincere. I guess we got caught up in catching up that I didn't realize that I had been gone for a bit. Drew excused himself so that he could make sure everything was alright with me. He ended up walking over to the hallway where Sean and I were talking, and saw Sean reach for my hand when I tried to leave for the washroom. Drew marched over pissed off and shouted, "Get your fucking hands off my girl. I'm pretty sure she mentioned me." Drew said stepping into Sean's face. "Or what are you going to do about it?" Sean said sounding brave. "Listen, this shit is not necessary. Sean I'll talk to you later.

Drew, baby, let's go, Trey and Cora are waiting," I said trying to stop the situation from getting out of hand. "Yeah, I would listen to your girl," Sean said to Drew as he pushed him. Drew turned around quickly and punched Sean dead in the face. Sean fell to the ground instantly. I called Trey to stop him from punching Sean repeatedly and he rushed over to pull Drew off of Sean. The manager came and we ran out of the restaurant. We got in our cars and drove off, headed to the movie theatre. Drew was still amped from the fight that we waited until he calmed down before walking towards the theatre. I grabbed onto his arm but Drew pulled away from me. I looked at him but he kept walking in front of me. I followed him in and he bought our tickets. As Cora and Trey got cozy in seats nearby, I asked Drew, "Are you mad at me? Sean and I are just friends." Drew ignored me and forced himself to look at the screen. I felt so uneasy with Drew acting so cold towards me. Seeing Trey and Cora all lovey-dovey made it even harder to accept Drew's sour behavior towards me.

After the movie, Cora and Trey said bye and left Drew and I. As Drew drove me home he said absolutely nothing. I tried to start up two separate conversations and was left to answer my own question. When we arrived at my house Drew finally found his voice, "I don't want you talking to that guy anymore." I could tell by the tone of his voice how serious he was. "How do you want me to do that? We have the same friends," I said to Drew. "When he comes around you should leave. I don't trust him around you," he answered without making eye contact. "You mean you don't trust me," I replied, slightly cutting him off. "Do you really think I would do anything to hurt you? I'm not Gina," I said sounding defensive. "Well you looked like you didn't mind the attention. You didn't pull your hand away when he was holding it, so what did you expect me to think?" After Drew said that, I tried to open the door to get out of the car. "I want to get out, unlock my door," I said calmly. Drew refused to unlock the door, "I'm not trying to start an argument, but I'm pissed that you had him feeling on you like that," Drew said as he tried to get his feelings across. "He touched my hand Drew, he wasn't feeling on my ass. You should trust me and know I would never do anything to hurt you. That's not how I was raised and I love you too much to jeopardize our relationship," I said to Drew letting my feelings be known. "I know, I should trust you, and I do; but these dudes out here, I just don't trust them. You're a beautiful girl Bonnie, guys are attracted to that. Some won't even care if you have a man, they'll still try to pursue you," Drew further explained. "You're right, but I can handle myself and these guys. You should never question your place in my life," I exclaimed. As we talked in my driveway I slid onto Drew's lap and began to kiss him slowly. "The way you handled Sean kind of turned me on," I whispered into his ear and gently kissed his ear lobe. "That turned you on? How bad did I turn you on?", Drew said softly on my neck. I moaned loudly as Drew pleasured me down below. I then saw a bright light coming through the back window of the car. I quickly jumped off Drew and we both hurried to fix ourselves. "Hi Bonnie. Hello Drew. What are you guys doing out here?", my dad said leaning down on the roof. Drew said hello sounding nervous and trying to hide his stiffness. "Hi daddy, Drew and I just got here. We went to the movies with Cora and her boyfriend Trey," I said to my dad as calmly as possible. "Alright. Good night you two," my dad said and went inside. Drew and I started dying of laughter. The fact that we almost got caught was scary but also a turn on. "I'm going to go inside now," I said to Drew. "So what? You're just going to leave me like this?" Drew pointed to the damage I've caused. I put my lips around his dick and sucked him slow, he threw his head back and moaned. I licked the tip and continued to blow him until he came. "Damn girl, you see why I was about to cut a dude." I laughed, gave him a kiss and went inside as Drew drove home with a big grin on his face.

A few days later, Donna called me out of the blue and invited me over to her place. I got ready and headed over that afternoon and we greeted each other with a hug. "What's up D?!", I said to Donna as I walked in her apartment. "Hi Bonnie!", she replied and seemed happy to have some company. "Where's the little cutie?", I asked. "I finally got her down for a nap. Do you want something to drink?" "No thanks Donna, I'm good. How's everything been going since living on your own?", I inquired. "It's good. Nelly has her own room; I don't have to deal with Pay and his bullshit. Plus, I'm seeing someone. His name is Roy, and he's a lot older than I am," Donna said. "How much older?", I asked. "He's 32, but before you say anything, he's really nice and he treats Nelly and I good," Donna said. "Does he have kids?" I asked curiously. "Yeah…Uhm…4 kids; 2 boys and 2 girls," Donna replied seemingly embarrassed. "Oh…Are they all by the same woman at least?", I asked. Donna looked away and mumbled, "No." "Come on Donna you can't be serious. You are using protection right? He clearly doesn't need any more baby mothers, and you clearly don't need to be just another baby mother," I scolded Donna. "I get your concern Bonnie, but Roy is a really good guy. He gives me money, buys groceries and has even paid a bill or two. He's a good guy Bonnie," Donna said trying to convince me. I didn't buy this at all. What would a 32-year-old man want with a 17-year-old girl? We were interrupted by a knock on her door. "What up baby," Roy grabbed Donna and kissed her aggressively. "Roy, this is my friend Bonnie," Donna introduced us. "What up pretty girl?", Roy greeted me. I couldn't help but give him screw face. "Hey," I replied. Nelly started crying so Donna went to go get her. "So how long have you and Donna been friends?", Roy asked me. "A couple of years," I answered showing complete disinterest in continuing on with the conversation. "You must be the prettiest of all Donna's friends, huh? Yeah, you're really pretty," Roy said sounding like a creep. Where did Donna find this perverted old man from? Donna is a pretty girl and would have no problem getting a guy. As much as I wanted to leave, I continued to chill with Donna a little longer, played with baby Nelly and we ordered Chinese food. Roy paid for it with bills from a roll of money in an elastic band he pulled out of his pocket. Roy ended up giving the delivery man a $40 tip because he didn't have any change. We ate food and had a few shots as the night rolled in. "Thank you for a good time Donna, but I think it's time for me head home." "How are you getting home?" Roy interrupted. "I'm taking a cab," I said to Roy. "Naw, it's too late for that. I'll drive you, I only had one beer." I was tipsy and just wanted to get home so I took Roy up on his offer. I gave Donna and Nelly a hug and kiss and left with Roy. The ride in the elevator was so uncomfortable; Roy was standing on the opposite side looking at me all creepy while licking his lips like he wanted to take a bite. We finally arrived at the lobby and walked outside over to where his car was parked. Roy was pushing a black Range Rover with 22-inch chrome rims. You could tell Roy was a show-off by the way he flaunted his material possessions. A few minutes in the car and I noticed that Roy kept looking at me. "Do I have something on my face?", I asked him in a rude sarcastic manner. "No. I'm just admiring your beauty," He said sounding like a perverted old man. "Well you need to stop because you're making me uncomfortable," I said bluntly. "I don't mean to make you uncomfortable, but you're a cute girl and I like that." I was so tired of this guy hitting on me; he's supposed to be my friend's man and he keeps making passes at me every chance he gets. "Let me out at the next bus stop, please," I demanded. "Bonnie, I'm just kidding," Roy said as he touched my thigh. We stopped at a red light and I unbuckled my seat belt and jumped out of his truck. "Bonnie?! Come on girl, you know I was just playing with you," Roy said yelling out the window. I didn't care. I refused to get back in the car with his creepy ass. Roy finally stopped trying to persuade me to get back in his ride and drove off. I hoped on the next bus home and called Cora to tell her what happened. She was disgusted when I told her the story and asked me if I told Donna. I told her that I would tell Donna tomorrow. Cora stayed on the phone with me to make sure I got home safely. When I finally arrived home safely, I told Cora and we planned to meet up the next day to get an outfit for the twins' party on the weekend. As I walked towards my house I saw Hazel's car in the driveway. I passed the car but no one was in it. I walked up to my front door and I pushed my key in the door. I saw my baby sister sitting in the living room watching television. "Hi Bonnie, Hazel's here." "Where?", I asked my sister. "In your room." I went upstairs to find Hazel sitting on my bed looking at pictures in my album. "Remember this night? It was Toni's party and his parents were out of town, the whole school was there and his house was a wreck when we left" Hazel said as she reminisced about our care-free days. "What are you doing here Hazel?", I asked wanting her to get to the point. I was still furious with Hazel and I wasn't sure if I could overlook what she had done this time. "I miss our friendship Bonnie. I know I messed up, plenty of times, but at this point in my life I really need a friend," Hazel said, pouring out her emotions. "Things have changed between us. You started dating Drew and then not being there for me as much..." I stopped Hazel before she continued, "What does Drew have to do with this? I've always been there for you before and since I've been with Drew. I just got tired of your bullshit. The secrets you keep and lies you tell are just too damaging, and I can't be a part of it anymore." I was fed up with Hazel and I didn't feel like I could continue to be her friend. "That's how you feel about me Bonnie? You think our whole friendship has been based on lies and my wrong doings," Hazel said as she became upset. "We've been best friends for years you're just willing to let go of our relationship like that? That's fucked up on your part. I thought we were best friends, but I guess I was wrong," Hazel concluded her rant. "You're so ungrateful Hazel. The fact that you have disregarded how I've treated you as a friend over the years because I've stopped running to your beckon call. If anyone's a fake friend, it's you! Tell me, what have you done to deserve a friend like me anyway? You haven't been there for me; and, you don't care about anyone but yourself," I yelled back at Hazel. By the look on Hazel's face, she was clearly shocked by the truth; and by the mean mug she was giving me, I knew that I would have to watch my back from this point forward. Hazel was very spiteful when she didn't get what she wanted. "Okay, it's cool. I know where we stand now Bonnie," Hazel said as she got up and left. As she was about to get inside her car, she made a call and looked up at my window. We made eye contact and she gave me a dirty look. It's not like I wanted things to end so ugly between us, but I guess that's how 'friendships' go sometimes.

Cora and I went shopping as planned the following day and I filled her in on Hazel and my argument at my house, before Drew and Trey came by to pick us up for dinner. "What did you lovely ladies buy?", Drew asked. "You have to wait and see tomorrow," I replied flirtatiously. We all got in the car and went to eat at Kelsey's. The whole time at dinner, Drew's phone kept vibrating, but what aggravated me most, was that Drew failed to even look at his phone. I looked at him waiting for him to answer it at least once, but he didn't. I didn't address the situation until later because I didn't want to cause a seen. Trey dropped Drew and I to my house after dinner and drove off with Cora. Drew tried to kiss me on my neck as we were walking inside, but I moved to redirect his kiss elsewhere. "What did I do now?", Drew sighed. "As if you already don't know. Why didn't you answer your phone at dinner? I know you heard it vibrating because the whole table did," I said rolling my eyes. "We were at dinner, wouldn't that have been rude of me?", Drew said thinking he was getting off easy. "The person called a dozen times. If anything was rude, it would be you not answering the phone. Obviously the call was important," I said to Drew digging him in a deeper hole. "Ok fine, it was Gina," Drew answered. "What? Why is she calling you? Why didn't you just tell me in the first place? Didn't we both make it clear to her that she is to leave us alone?", I asked Drew one question after another with major attitude. "I know, but her grandmother died and because I was close with her when we use to be together, she thought I would like to know," Drew replied. Drew has a big heart and people will use that against him. I know it would be selfish for me to not want Drew to attend her funeral, but I just don't trust Gina. She tried to break up our relationship before, and who's to believe that she wouldn't try to do it again. "I just don't trust that girl Drew. She has to be up to something, I know it," I expressed my concern to Drew. "I know baby, but I was close with her family and it would be a bit rude of me if I didn't attend the funeral tomorrow to show my support. I'll make it back in time to go to Jenelle and Jayna's party." I was pissed off, but I managed to put my anger aside due to the circumstances. "Ok, but make sure that bitch is 20 feet away from you or else I will have to kill the both of you," I said trying to lighten the mood. Drew laughed as we walked inside my house. I noticed it was 12 o'clock, so I called Jayna and Jenelle to wish them a happy birthday. "Happy birthday girlies!", I yelled at the top of my lungs. "Thanks Bonnie! You are coming to our party tomorrow, right?" Jenelle asked. "Of course, I wouldn't miss it for the world!" Jayna and Jenelle sounded happy and drunk out of their minds. I told the girls good night and then called a cab for Drew. "Babe, have you seen my shirt?", Drew asked. "It's right here," I said placing it between my legs. We managed to get a quickie in before the cab came

I took a shower and played some music as I got dressed the following evening for the Twinzys birthday bash. I wore my hair in a high ponytail showing off my diamond studs and tennis bracelet I got from my mom on my sweet sixteen. About half an hour later Cora showed up to get me for the party. Looking of age, we stopped to get some liquor as we knew we wouldn't get ID. We made another stop to pick up some blunts from our weed man and then made it to the Twinzys condo party. We went upstairs to their apartment first and then went out on the rooftop where the party was. It wasn't even 10 o'clock and the place was packed. The DJ was playing the latest tunes and had everyone up on their feet dancing. There was liquor and weed on the table ready for our indulgence. Jayna and Jenelle were dressed to impress looking like they hit the lotto. They were having a good time and were most definitely the wildest ones at the party. Cora and I were on the dance floor with a drink in one hand and a blunt in the other. Just as we were having a great time, Hazel walked through the door. She looked nice and she dyed her hair burgundy red which she wore long and straight. She walked over to the Twinzys to wish them a happy birthday and then headed over to Study. It seemed like she was trying to avoid me the way Study was trying to avoid her. Study had brought Desha with him and had been telling Crystal and Cora that he wanted to call it off with Hazel. All of a sudden Study built a conscious about cheating on Desha. I guess Study hadn't found a way to tell Hazel, so now he was trying to keep his distance and give her the cold shoulder. Hazel clearly seemed to be missing the point though, because she was everywhere Study went, but when Desha came around she would leave and go stand across the room and just watch him. We were 2 hours into the party, and Hazel and I still hadn't said one word to each other. I noticed her on her phone a lot, she kept going where there weren't a lot of people so she could do her dirt in private. "What time is Drew coming?", Cora asked. "I'm not too sure. I've been trying to call him but I can't get a hold of him yet," I replied. I was getting worried as I knew he was around that slut Gina, but I needed to trust him, even though him not picking up his phone at dinner the previous night made me question his honesty. As the night rolled on I forgot about Drew not being there and I got so drunk that I finally built up the courage to go and talk to Hazel to see where things stood between us. I saw her flirting with Pay in a corner; I guess because she wasn't getting any attention from Study. Before I could walk over to her, Hazel left the rooftop and I followed behind her. Hazel was talking on her phone again that she didn't notice I was there so I tried to stay quiet to see if I knew who she was talking to. "Hey, are you still at the funeral?", Hazel asked the person on her other end. "Is he drunk?...Do you think you could get a picture of him doing something incriminating?" I was starting to put two and two together. "I just don't want him around my friend anymore. Drew needs to go. She spends all her time with him and that has jeopardized our relationship," I overheard Hazel clear as day. I was shocked and so furious. "I don't care Gina, every guy cheats, now make it happen," Hazel blurted out. I charged over to Hazel and pushed her from behind. "You Bitch!", I yelled. I started punching her until she threw me off of her and punched me back. We were fighting each other like men, none of that pulling hair or slapping girl shit. This was real. I managed to get off the floor and kick Hazel in her back. I put her in a choke hold. "You fucking bitch! How could you do this? Does our friendship mean nothing to you?", I asked her as I continued to keep her in the choke hold. Cora and Trey must have been coming inside to find a room or something, but if they didn't come that second I would have killed Hazel. They broke us apart and I spit on Hazel while Trey grabbed me by the waist and lifted me up away from her on the ground. "Fuck you! Don't ever talk to me again! Don't call me! Stay the fuck away from me!", I screamed at Hazel with every ounce of anger I had. I left the party with Cora and Trey so pissed off that I didn't even say bye to Jayna and Jenelle. The whole party heard about Hazel and my fight, but I didn't care. I called

Drew and told him to leave the funeral and let him know what Hazel and Gina were plotting. When I was on the phone with him, I heard Gina begging him for his forgiveness, saying it wasn't her fault and it was all Hazel's idea. I shouted through the phone, "When I see you, it's on Bitch!" Drew cussed her before he left. Drew said he would meet me at his house so Trey dropped me off. I cried all the way there, I was so hurt. How could my best friend do this to me? I've been nothing but a good friend to get her and she stabbed me in the back like she did everyone else. When we got to Drew's house I told Trey to take Cora home and waited for Drew. I saw the same white Honda pull up, I thought it was Gina, so I stood up and rolled my fist ready to fight but Drew came out the car instead. "The bitch threw my car keys when I tried to leave so I had to take her car," Drew said to me. By the time we started to walk inside 2 police cars rolled up. "Are you Drew?" one of the officer's asked. "Yes," Drew responded. "You're under arrest," the officer said to Drew as they put him in handcuffs. I begged the officer not to take him away and tried to tell them why he had her car but they wouldn't listen. "Go and get my mom and tell her what's going on. Meet me at the station later with our lawyer," Drew said as they placed him in the back of their cruiser. I ran inside and told Drew's mom what happened. She made one phone call and within minutes her lawyer was at the station. I told their lawyer what happened and he said that he wouldn't be able to get him out tonight but that he would definitely work something out for the morning. I was worried for Drew, but I had to stay clear-headed and hope for the best. Once everything was straightened out I would deal with Gina and Hazel accordingly.

CHAPTER 19: EVERY DOG HAS THEIR DAY

Twelve hours later, Drew's lawyer finally got him released from police custody. "Are you ok baby?", I asked. "Yeah, I'm alright. You were right about that girl, Bonnie. She fucked me over big time," Drew replied shaking his head. Drew's mother walked over to us. "Drew, I told you about Gina. I never liked her. We need to do something about this before it gets worse," she scolded. We left the police station together, and Drew dropped me home.

By the time I got home and tried to get some sleep, my phone started going off with messages from my girls and some other people I talk to on a regular. I wasn't in the mood to be interrogated, so I switched my phone to silent mode and fell asleep immediately. As much as I was trying to focus on moving forward, the reality of people closest to me going out of their way just to hurt me was mind boggling. Things have changed drastically between my friends and I, but I believe everything happens for a reason.

I woke up around 8 o'clock that evening to more missed calls and text messages on my phone. I got up and went downstairs to watch a movie with my family and then decided to head back to bed once it was over. I called Cora back first to fully explain the fight between Hazel and myself, and to inform her of Hazel's part in Leena's death and how Roy was blackmailing her for sex. After talking with Cora for about two hours, I decided to call Donna. I had to let her know that Roy was a creep and she needed to ditch him fast. "Hey Donna, I have something to tell you," I said to Donna. She interrupted, "I know, I heard what happened last night at the twins' party. Why did you and Hazel fight?" "I filled her in even though the fight between Hazel and myself was not the something I wanted to tell her. "That's not what I called to talk about," I said and told her all about Roy and how uncomfortable he made me feel. "He was just joking Bonnie. It's not that serious, he flirts with everybody," Donna responded trying to justify Roy's actions. "I don't think he was joking Donna. He was persistent, so much that I had to jump out of his truck as soon as he stopped at a red light," I exclaimed to Donna. "I know Roy and he cares about me so just drop it Bonnie," Donna insisted. "No Donna, I'm not going to just drop it. I watched Pay treat you like shit and now this guy is taking advantage of you too," I said to Donna trying to convince her of what a dog Roy is. "How come you weren't so eager to tell me when Pay was fucking our friend?", Donna snapped at me. "I... I should have told you. I am sorry for not telling you and watching you be made a fool of. I had to find out the hard way about Hazel and I could only imagine how you felt, but I'm just trying to make things right. I don't want to see you get hurt again." I tried to get Donna to understand that I was coming from a good place. "I don't want to hear it Bonnie. You can't pick and choose when you want to be my friend. Hazel had to screw you over in order for you to realize she wasn't a true friend. How does it feel getting the shit end of the stick now?", Donna asked. "All I was trying to do was help you. You have all right to be mad at me, but why let this get in the way of the truth I'm speaking right now? Roy's a jerk and you're going to realize it when it's too late. I don't want that for you." "All of a sudden you and Hazel are no longer friends so now you care to be a real friend to me. Fuck you Bonnie!" Donna said before hanging up the phone. I was appalled and surprised. I know Donna said she forgave me, but I didn't realize how deep her pain was. I didn't only lose Hazel as a friend, but I lost Donna too and I was partly to blame. I should have never stood up for Hazel keeping such a damaging secret, and I should not have not waited until Hazel betrayed me in order to see her for the

123

jealous, manipulative person she is. She never wanted good for the people around her unless she was doing better, she was jealous and always felt the attention should be on her all of the time. Before my head even touched my pillow my phone rang, it was Hazel. I couldn't believe she had the audacity to call me. There was nothing she could say to make things better, and there was no going back to the friends we use to be. She must have called two more times before sending me a text: 'We should talk.' I didn't reply. I don't owe Hazel anything, she messed up for the last time and there was no fixing it.

The next morning I woke and got ready for school. With all the drama that was going on, I was leaning more and more towards going with Drew to NY to stay with his sister for a few weeks out of the summer. First and second period helped me get my mind off all the drama for a bit, but when I walked in the cafeteria at lunch and saw Donna with a smirk on her face, I just prepared myself for a showdown. All of a sudden all the lights went out and an image of three people having sex was projected on the wall. It was Hazel's sex tape! Everybody was watching, including Hazel. I couldn't believe Ray actually leaked the video. If he wanted to tell the school he had sex with Hazel fine, but Leena died not too long ago, and it wasn't right for him to put this out, this is not the way she should be remembered. The video showed them doing drugs and was exactly what Hazel described. Tears ran down Hazel's face and she ran out the cafeteria. By the time the teachers turned the video off, everyone had already seen enough to gossip about. The bigger shock was to find out that the video tape wasn't leaked by Ray, but by Donna. Donna managed to get her hands on the tape because her cousin used to mess around with Ray. When the Principal got hold of the news, Donna was expelled immediately. No one had any remorse for Hazel; as a matter of fact, they made her last days of high school a living hell. People didn't only laugh at her, but they called her a killer. Donna wasn't found to be any better considering she was Leena's friend; but apparently what pushed her over the edge was that Hazel was still messing with Pay and that Caleb was his son. Donna found out because Pay sent Donna a text message that he meant to send to Hazel; I guess it's true that every dog has their day.

I called a cab and headed over to Drew's house after school. When I got there, Drew was sitting on his stoop waiting for me. He paid the driver and opened my door. I kissed him embracing him tightly, "I missed you!" "I know," He said sarcastically. "You know I've missed you and that butt of yours," Drew said gripping a palm full of my ass as we went inside. I said hello to Drew's mother and sister and asked Drew's mother how she was feeling. I know she wants nothing but the best for Drew, and now having to take time out to deal with the mess with Gina became an unnecessary burden for her to bear. "I'm trying to stay relaxed. The lawyer has a good case for Drew's defence," His mom said. "That's good to hear," I replied with a smile. Drew and I headed upstairs to his room to spend a quiet night in just relaxing and watching movies.

Drew and I wrapped up our date and he took me home. We made out a little before I went inside, but when Drew pulled out of my driveway and drove off, I saw Gina's white Honda pull up. "Yo!" Gina yelled out the driver's window. "You have a lot of nerve showing your face around here. I should beat your ass right now just like I beat up you partner in crime," I said aggressively to Gina. Fearless, I walked closer to her vehicle. "Drew has to go to court because of your lying ass and you say you care about him? Now he has to deal with this shit because of you," I informed Gina the negative affect her antics had caused. "Listen Bonnie, that wasn't my intension. It was all innocent at first, but it did go too far. I want Drew back but I know that with everything that has happened and just by his actions that Drew really loves you and there's no changing that. I just didn't want to accept it…" I was shocked to hear Gina come with her half ass apology, but it was big of her and I respected her for it. "That friend of yours is not a real friend," Gina warned me, as if I didn't figure that out for myself. "I know, and she's no longer my friend," I told Gina sounding stand offish. "Well, that's all I wanted to say. Again, I'm sorry," Gina said as she drove off. I went inside puzzled but relieved. I called Drew once I got inside and told him what happened. He was as surprised as I was.

Exam week started and I was ready to knock them down, one by one. I didn't want anything to ruin my chances of passing my courses and getting into the Universities of my choice. The day before my last exam Drew called, "Hey baby, you're not going to believe what happened? Gina dropped the charges! I guess she finally wised up and realized that my heart is yours to keep." I could hear the relief in Drew's voice. "I'm so happy to hear that. That's the best news I've heard in a while," I replied. "You should take me out to celebrate," Drew said in a playful way. "Oh, I'll give you something to eat," I said flirting back. Drew and I talked some more until I had to cut the conversation short to study for my last exam. The following day I wrote my last exam with ease. I was thrilled to celebrate my last day of high school, and even more excited to leave the drama behind. I said farewell to a couple of my classmates and the teachers who had a positive impact on me, and burned a blunt with Ziggy at the stoners' corner for old times.

CHAPTER 20: ENDINGS BRING NEW BEGINNINGS

It felt like a new beginning. I was feeling free from all the drama in my life. No more Hazel and her sneaky ways, and Donna unfriended me but I was fine with that. In a way, I felt like I deserved it, but she did act shady in regards to the sex tape and the way she went about her true feelings towards me after I told her about her sleazy boyfriend. If she didn't want to be my friend after the Pay and Hazel incident I could respect that, but instead she pretended to be my friend for selfish reasons. I would rather be alone than be around a bunch of people around that I need to constantly have my guard up around. The one person I knew I could count on was Cora. We think alike and truly value one another's friendship, and now that summer was finally here I planned on enjoying my new drama free life. I called up Jayna to see if they were home and she said to come by, so I swung over there to see how they were doing and if they wanted to come to the dinner party with the rest of us. When I got there Jenelle opened the door and all I could feel was a bad vibe off her. "Hey Jenelle", I said. "Hey," she responded back. I shut the door behind me and went inside. Jenelle went to her room and I saw Crystal, Jayna and of course Hazel on the couch. We made eye contact but didn't utter a word to one another. She got up and went on the balcony for a smoke. I looked at Jayna, "Why didn't you tell me she was going to be here?" "Cause you didn't ask," Jayna said with an attitude. I said hello to Crystal and sat down. Jenelle came out of her room and proceeded towards us, Hazel then came back in. "You guys need to talk," Jenelle said looking more towards me like it was my fault. "I don't need or want to talk to that girl. She's the one that went and started something from nothing and due to that, we are no longer friends," I said loud and clear. "And what the heck is this? An intervention? I'm not the one that needs help. I only came over here to ask if my two friends wanted to come to my grad dinner, but now I have to have a sit down with this heffer? Hell nah, peace," I stated. Hazel kissed her teeth while Crystal looked like she felt very uncomfortable being present to this awkward situation. "Bonnie, I think you're being unreasonable. You and Hazel have been..." I interrupted Jayna quick, "I don't want to hear about how long we have been friends. That shit didn't mean anything to her when she fucked Pay behind Donna's back putting all of us in the middle between our loyalty to her and Donna; or when she plotted with Drew's ex to sabotage our relationship; or when she let Ray blackmail her into sleeping with him in order to keep her part in Leena's death a secret! You guys need to drop this. Don't wait until it happens to you. If you guys are smart, drop her now," I warned Jayna and Jenelle. I have never gotten into it with the Twinzys before today, but I was starting to see where our relationship was headed. It seemed like Jenelle had some hard feelings towards Hazel after the video came out, but she seemed to gravitate to Hazel more after our falling out. Jayna was iffy, she had an opinion but she didn't seem like she cared much. I preferred that she didn't too because I didn't need to hear anybody else trying to force me into being Hazel's friend again. "Listen, if you want to come to my grad night the invitation still stands. I'm done with whatever this is," I said and then walked off letting myself out. I hopped on the next bus back home.

It was the day before my graduation and I was feeling so good. I got up to smoke a morning spliff to start my day off right and as I walked out onto my balcony, I saw a nice white Jeep truck with a bow on it. By the time I turned around to run inside to say thank you to my parents, my mom and dad were standing right in front of the front door with the keys to my new ride. I jumped on my dad and gave my mom the biggest hug and kiss. "You're welcome baby," my dad said as I hugged him again. "Come let me take my fam bam for a spin," I said excited. I took them for a drive around the block. My mom already had my favourite CD in the car, she knew how much I love my Rihanna. When we got back home, I thanked my parents again before they all got out of my new car. I decide to pay a quick visit to Cora to show her my new whip. I called her outside and she started screaming. "Damn Bonnie, that's you? That baby is nice!", she said. We sat in the car and explored all its features. We then went inside of her house to light my morning spliff that was interrupted due to all the excitement. We smoked, talked a little and I took her for another spin. I told Cora about Jayna and Jenelle and what they tried to do yesterday. "Well I spoke with them late last night and reminded them about your graduation dinner tonight. If they come then just work it out with them, and if they don't, then you know what your friendship status is," Cora advised me. After our talk, I drove home and made my family and I breakfast before handing my mom a few envelopes from the schools I applied to that had come to a decision regarding my future. As she was opening them for me, nerves took over my body. "What if I got rejected from all of them? What if I've been waitlisted mom?" My mother sat me down beside her and said, "Here, you open them Bonnie." I opened them up one by one before pulling them out. I turned them over at the same time. I quickly skimmed through the words to find out that I was accepted by 2 out of the 3 schools that I applied for. I was thrilled because out of the 2 that I was accepted to, I got the one I was hoping for- George Brown College, I decided to take the business program there. My family was so thrilled for me. I was very proud of myself; graduating from high school, getting accepted into College, and weeding out unnecessary and toxic people in my life. I was in a positive place and I was liking the new changes.

Drew took me out to Woodbine Casino with Cora and Trey, and we ate at one of the restaurants nearby first. Trey, who I even formed a great bond with through all of the drama over the past year, paid for everything. We hit the slots after dinner and I ended up winning $3,000 on the tables. We all had a good time and enjoyed each other's company with good vibes throughout the entire night. We hit up a club downtown and partied the night away. We had bottles rolling in and great music to accompany the vibe. I didn't get home until 5 in the morning. Drew came inside for a night cap, minus the night cap. We didn't even make it upstairs to my room. We slept right on the living room floor. With all that liquor in us, there was no shame in what we did.

Last night was one for the books, and today wasn't just my graduation, it was the day I put an end to the past that I eagerly wanted to leave behind. I was excited but I wanted to close this chapter in my life and see what was next to unfold. I never thought that things would be the way they are with the people I felt would always be in my life, but everything happens for a reason. I got ready for my graduation ceremony, and Drew met me at my house and we all drove in a limo together. Cora and Trey were going to meet us there for the ceremony.

When we arrived, it was packed with ambitions young adults of the future. Some were there to make a difference in the world, others just wanted to prove something to their parents, and the rest barely made it through; but the one thing we all had in common, was that we made it! Regardless of how we got to this point in our lives, we were all here for a special occasion. As the evening progressed they called our names. When Hazel was called to receive her Diploma the entire school booed her off the stage. Donna would have loved to see that, but she was expelled before she could graduate. I heard that her creep boyfriend has been beating her and cheating on her; but regardless of Donna and my friendship, it was sad to

130

hear that being that Donna has a little girl that has to be objected to that. I wished her the best. When they called my name my family and friends cheered me on. The look on their faces showed how proud they were of me as I walked across the stage and received my Diploma. I looked at everyone and said to myself, this will be the last time I will see some of their faces and that was fine with me. I walked off the stage feeling like I had completed my first true journey and only hoped for many more to come, minus all the drama. After we all received our Diplomas, we raised our hats and threw them in the air as we cheered. We hugged each other and cried as we got ready for adulthood over the summer when the real world would hit most of us. After the ceremony, my family, Drew and I went out to celebrate. They told me again how proud they were of me, and my sisters gave me a gift from Tiffany's, "We bought it with our allowance." "Thanks dolls," I said almost in tears as I put on the charm bracelet they picked out with me in mind. We finished our dinner and headed home, but not before they surprised me with a red velvet cheese cake – my favourite dessert! Drew and I said goodnight and he waited for me to get in before getting into his car. My parents and sisters went to bed and I headed to the bathroom to run a bubble bath and listen to some Usher before bed, but before I could get into the water my phone rang. "Open the door," Drew said and hung up. I went downstairs quietly in my robe and opened the door. Drew came in and he kissed me on my lips, as he shut the door behind him. I proceeded to lead him upstairs. "I'm so proud of you baby," Drew said to me as he held me and whispered in my ear. "Thank you," I replied. As soon as we got in my room, Drew undid my robe and just looked at my body. He then placed his hands around my waist, running his hands down my hips as he drew me in closer. I undid his zipper and slid them off along with his boxers. I pulled his shirt over his head and kissed his neck passionately. Drew and I made our way into the tub to relax. As I lay between his legs, we enjoyed our wine

I borrowed from my dad's collection and each other's company. We talked about school and me going to NY with him for a few weeks. "I decided to go to George Brown for Business. I know we talked about us going to the same school, but I don't want us to get tired of each other," I whispered to Drew. "I respect your decision," Drew responded with a kiss on the back of my head. I was happy he understood. We were excited for a change of scenery and to explore NYC for a bit. We talked until the sun started to rise and then Drew got up to go home. I felt fulfilled and satisfied from my special day with my family and my love.

The following day I booked my ticket to NYC, and since my dad gave me some graduation money to upgrade me closet, Cora and I decided to meet up to do just that. I picked Cora up and we ate lunch and chatted before going shopping. She told me that her and Trey decided to move in together and buy a condo close to downtown Toronto. I was happy for her. Trey and her came along way since the abortion. They were back on the right track. After we finished shopping we headed to my Jeep and just as Cora and I were walking out, we saw Jenelle and Jayna. While Jayna gave us a head nod, Jenelle didn't say or make any kind of gesture. Cora looked at me and laughed, "They weren't at your party to celebrate a milestone that was meaningful to you, and it's not like they had a reason not to be there for you to show their support. That means they don't need to be in your life." Cora was right, and neither of us sweated the small stuff anymore. We laughed and talked all the way home. I dropped Cora off at Trey's and went home to pack.

The week had gone by so quickly that it was already time for Drew and I to go on our trip to New York City- the city that never sleeps. I went home after picking up some last minute items from Shoppers Drug Mart, did my laundry and packed my bags for my flight the next day. I called Drew and talked to him while I got everything together. "Babe what should I bring?", I asked. "That ass and your pretty smile," Drew said charmingly. I laughed. After I got my bags packed Drew and I gave each other a kiss over the phone and said we will see each other tomorrow. I cleaned up my room and got myself organized before going to bed.

The next day my dad made me breakfast and had a talk with me before he left for work. "You know Bonnie, you're my oldest daughter and I love you very much. I want you to be safe and responsible," he preached to me in concern that I may get pregnant. "I know daddy, and I will. I will call you as soon as I arrive and I'll check in every so often," I said to my dad reassuring him that I had a good head on my shoulders and was focused on my career. My dad gave me a kiss on my forehead and gave me an envelope of cash before leaving for work. I went to chill out with my mom and siblings before it was time for me to go. We did a little last minute shopping, enjoyed a late lunch and said our goodbyes before they dropped me off at Cora's house to meet up with Drew. "I'm going to miss you Bonnie!", Cora said as we hugged each other tightly. "Aww, don't worry bestie I'll be back before you know it!", I replied. Trey got to Cora's house around 6:00 p.m. with Drew. Our flight was leaving at eight. So we packed our suitcases in Trey's car and headed to the airport. Drew and I were cuddled up in the backseat. I was thrilled that we were leaving the country together. When we arrived at the airport Cora was in tears. "You better not make any new best friends in NY!", Cora said sarcastically. "You know no one could take your spot," I said as I gave her the biggest hug. "Don't worry Cora, you have me to keep you company," Trey said with a smile on his face. Cora jokingly gave him a look as if he wasn't enough. Drew and I started laughing. Trey and Drew said their goodbyes and we left to get on our flight. After checking our bags in, and all the security checks, Drew and I were finally boarding our flight. "This feels good," Drew mentioned as he placed his arm around me. "Yes it does!", I added. I knew from here on out that my future was going to be brighter and that I had a lot to look forward to.